UNTIL

TANNER CYCLES

Sydney

MARISSA DOBSON

Published by Dobson Ink
Printed in the United States of America
ISBN-13: 978-1-939978-96-7

Dedication:

To my husband, Thomas, the love of my life.

Love deserves a chance…

Contents

Chapter One

Outside the office windows, the world went by unnoticed by Coal Tanner as he continued working late into the night. Work didn't stop just because the day faded into darkness. He put his heart and soul into Tanner Cycles and his work was never done. There were always parts to be found and ordered, clients to contact, designs to be approved, and more. The business had exploded far beyond what he'd thought it would. While that meant he had to take on more of an administrative role, leaving the hands-on work to his brothers, he still received the same rush of adrenaline with each completed project.

His cell phone vibrated along his desk, stealing his attention from the computer screen. *Unknown caller.* For a moment, he debated not answering it. The only people who had his number were his brothers, and a few friends. Business calls went to his office phone first and if he wasn't there, they would be directed to his cell phone. This call never came through his office, meaning it was either someone close to him or a wrong number. With everyone's number that was important to him programmed into the phone, it was more likely the latter. Still, he found himself putting his work on hold and picking up the call.

"Hello?"

"Fuck, man, I thought you weren't going to answer."

"Jay?" Coal's original frustration fizzled out as the voice of his old buddy drifted through the speaker. "How's it going?"

"Not so good. I was locked up tonight, but that's not why I called." Jay paused for a moment and lowered his voice. "It's Syd."

"Fuck, man!" He dragged his hand through his hair and leaned back in his leather office chair. "Tell me you didn't get her involved in your shit." It was bad enough that his old buddy couldn't clean his act up but to bring his sister down with him took the whole mess to another level.

"Nah, but she's in trouble. If they can't find me…" Jay hesitated. "You know what will happen. Fuck! You've got to help me. That's my baby sister."

Yeah, he knew what would happen. They'd go after anyone connected to him, which would leave Sydney with a bullseye on her back that she might not even know about. "Where is she? Still living at your old house?"

"Yeah. I know it's a few hours' drive from you, but I don't have anyone else to call that can keep her safe."

"What about your dad? Can't he watch out for her?" With the mention of Mr. Manor, Coal's chest tightened. He didn't like the idea of Syd being alone with him, even if he was her father. Whenever he was strung out on drugs, he turned abusive and Coal wouldn't force anyone to suffer that torment, especially not Syd.

"He's been locked up for a couple years now. Guess I'll be joining him…" There was noise on the other end and Jay's voice rose a notch. "I'm begging, man—you've got to help her."

"Don't sweat it. I'm heading out now. She's not going to be happy, but I'll have to bring her up here with me. It's the best way to protect her. I can't be gone from the shop for months." Coal hit the save button on the document he was working on and shut down the laptop.

"I don't give a shit if you drag her away kicking and screaming. Just protect her. If anything happens to her—"

The line went dead and Coal tossed the phone back onto the desk. No doubt his time was up. Coal didn't need Jay to finish the threat for him to know his friend would hold him responsible if anything happened to Syd. Jay wouldn't place the blame on himself for getting into this mess and leaving Sydney at risk. He would only see Coal's inability to protect her.

Coal would drop everything to make sure she was safe. It didn't matter, because there was no way he was letting her get caught up in the shit her brother left her in the middle of.

Shoving his laptop into his bag, he glanced at the clock on the wall, realizing it was past midnight. "Fuck." It would take him at least twelve hours in the car, and that was with him breaking the speed limit and not hitting any traffic. He needed to get there quick if he was going to get her out of town before whoever Jay owed money to came looking for him. He grabbed his cell phone off his desk again and scrolled through his contacts. *Knuckles.*

The late hour didn't faze him as he hit the button to call his old friend. Knuckles was a good guy, loyal to the family, and had been their pilot for more than ten years. There wasn't a doubt in Coal's mind that he could trust him to be willing to jump his aid now.

"Yeah?"

"Knuckles, I need a lift. How soon can you make it to the airstrip?"

"Tonight?" There was a hush of a female voice in the background, letting Coal know that Knuckles wasn't alone. "Fine, man. Give me twenty. Will I be waiting for you? I have another run tomorrow afternoon, so I need to be back before then."

"No, just drop me off in Pittsburgh. Then you can return, get some sleep, and be ready for Cal. File the flight plan. I'll see you when you get here." He didn't give Knuckles a chance to respond before hitting end on the cell phone and placing it back on the desk. Who knew how long it would take him to convince Sydney she needed to get out of town? He wouldn't hold Knuckles up when his brother, Callaway, needed him to pick up a cycle from Texas they were going to restore.

He left his laptop bag sitting by his desk and headed up the steps to his place. While his brothers shared a house on the other side of the landing strip, he preferred his privacy, so he'd turned the third floor of the warehouse into his own private condo. It had been used for storage but with some time, money, and a lot of cleaning, it had turned into a sanctuary where he could get away from work, at least as much as he would allow himself. He'd gather a few things in case he got tied up in Pennsylvania and once they were in the air, he'd arrange for a rental car.

Flying out of Pittsburgh's airport with Syd would be too risky. Too many people could see them traveling through the terminals. He'd need to get her out of the city, possibly out of the state, before they could risk Knuckles flying them back to Minnesota. By then it would be easier to just continue the trip back by car, rather than wait for Knuckles. *Especially if she's fighting me every step of the way.*

Every step Sydney Manor took in the old house produced a creak that seemed more sinister now that she was alone. It wasn't the first time in her life she had been home alone, but this *was* the first time no one would be coming back to her. She was alone in the world and finding someone on the porch when she arrived home from work had left her uneasy. It was a friend of Jay's but his cryptic warning told her he'd be trouble.

Terrified, she made sure every door and window was locked, before escaping to what had once been her sanctuary—her room. She needed to figure some things out. With her father and two brothers behind bars, how was she going to pay the bills, handle whatever legal fees they needed, and everything else? She needed to come up with a plan. Instead, all she could think was that she was the last Manor standing. All of the males in her family had ventured down the wrong route in life, while she'd vowed to stay out of trouble and away from the drugs that had ruined her family.

Maybe she needed to leave the area. The part of town they lived in had become so consumed by drugs and crime, it wasn't safe there any longer— especially not without Jay or someone there. At eighteen having just graduated from high school a couple of months ago, surely she could find work somewhere else. A hundred bucks was all she had to her name, but there had to be something in this shit hole they called home that she could sell.

A fist pounded on the door, and fear rose within her. Without turning on a light, she reached over to her nightstand and grabbed the handgun she had placed there. The gun was her father's, but he'd taught her how to use it years ago. He must have known he was going to prison and she'd be left with Jay. This had been his gift to her, so she could protect herself if the time ever came. Her brother had been into the same shit as her father so he had to realize that one day this would be her fate. They'd sheltered her, protecting her from the worst parts of their lives. Now, something about this whole situation screamed that she had been tossed directly into shark infested waters. What was she supposed to do?

The pounding on the door stopped, then resumed; whoever it was had gone to the back door. She wanted to creep out of her room and see who it could be but whoever was there in the middle of the night hadn't come for a visit. They were coming because of something Jay had done. She didn't want to die because he owed someone money, or someone wanted drugs.

The hundred dollars she had in her purse was all she had. She couldn't pay someone off.

The noise subsided and her breaths came easier. The person at the door would be back, though; she wasn't going to get rid of her problems that easy. Knowing that she needed to get out of there, she eased off the bed and began to throw things into a duffle bag. There was no place to go but she couldn't stay. She had to do something.

"Sydney." The male voice was unfamiliar.

The stairs creaked and she pressed her back to her bedroom wall. She held the gun out before her, knowing she needed to relax, focus on the target, and be ready when he entered her room.

"Syd..." The soft, husky voice drifted through the door.

It can't be. Maybe it was her ears playing tricks on her but she swore that voice belonged to someone she knew. Someone she could trust. With the gun at the ready, she couldn't stop the dash of hope from blooming within her. Could he have known and come for her? All these years later, would he be her saving grace again?

Without a sound, the bedroom door handle turned and the door drifted open. Could she do this? Could she really pull the trigger? She didn't know but her finger hovered over it. *Give me the strength...*

"Syd..." A man stepped through the open door and her heart skipped a beat.

"Coal!" Tears streamed from her eyes. She wanted to go to him and have him wrap his arms around her, but fear rooted her to the spot. How did he know she needed him?

"Damn it, why didn't you answer me!"

"What do you want?" Suspicion crept into her words. Was he tied into the mess Jay was in? She knew he and his brothers had left the state and made it big but it didn't stop the misgiving from tainting her thoughts.

What was the big man behind Tanner Cycles doing slumming in her neck of the woods? Now that he was a rich man, he never came back to their old stomping grounds.

"Syd." He stepped farther into the room. "I came for you. Get your stuff. We're going somewhere safe."

"I can't..." She didn't know why she said that. While she had dreamed about him coming and rescuing her from the mess she called her life, now that he was here, she was scared. But did she fear leaving everything she knew behind or her feelings for him? She wasn't sure. He could have any woman he wanted. Why would he want her?

"Can't?" He tipped his head toward the half packed duffle bag on her bed. "It looks like you were considering just that when I arrived."

"They're after me." Her gaze drifted toward the window as she wondered if they were outside. Were they out there waiting for her to come out? Would they eventually make their way inside and find her? She couldn't stay cooped up in the house forever. She'd have to go grocery shopping; after all, there was nothing left in the refrigerator expected a sour container of milk and Chinese food from three days ago. *Damn you, Jay!*

"I know. That's why I'm here." Watching her intently, he inched closer to her. "How about we put down the gun?"

"Huh?" She followed his gaze and realized she was still pointing the gun at his chest. "Shit!" Carefully moving her finger away from the trigger, she lowered it. In her heart, she knew she couldn't shoot Coal, even if it turned out he was part of Jay's mess.

"Give it to me." He held his hand out for it.

"I might need it." There was no safety on the gun and she already had one round ready in the chamber, just in case. "They were already here."

He closed the distance between them and with one hand, he cupped the side of her face, while with the other, he reached for the gun that she now pointed at the floor. "Do you trust me, Sydney?"

"Yes." The single word came out more like a squeak as she could finally take in the man before her. Before the darkness and shadows prevented her from getting a good look at him. The pictures in the magazines and online didn't do him justice. His broad shoulders and thick biceps made her feel small. She wanted to reach around his neck and unravel the tie that kept his shoulder length, dark brown hair out of his face. In the years since he'd left the city, he'd transformed from a young man with an attitude to a man who was beyond sexy.

"Syd, are you listening to me?" He took the gun from her hand and placed it on the dresser.

"What?" She blinked away her thoughts and the anxiety rushed back. "I, umm…"

"Finish packing. We're leaving." He stepped back from her and she had to wrap her arms around herself to shake off the chill.

"I don't have anywhere to go." Even as she argued, she went to her dresser, pulling out the few things she wanted to take with her.

"You're coming home with me." He stepped to the window and glanced out at the street. "Take everything you need. You won't be coming back here for a while, if ever."

She tossed the last of her clothes into the bag before grabbing her purse and the money she'd hidden from Jay in her nightstand. "Maybe Jay will get out and…"

"I doubt it." He stepped back from the window and nodded to the bag. "Ready?"

"Why do you doubt it?" While she could take a guess, she wasn't even sure what he'd been arrested for. "He has to come back." If he didn't get out of jail and take care of whoever was looking for her, how would she be able to move on with her life? Wouldn't they continue looking for her, until he squared things with them? She wasn't sure if he owed them drugs or money but she had no doubt he owed them big for them to already be at the house looking for him.

"Syd..." As his gaze fell on her, the words faded away, and sadness shined back at her when she looked him in the eyes. "Fuck! I could kill him for putting you in the middle of this."

"It's bad, isn't it?" The pieces of the puzzle were falling into place and she realized it was worse than she thought. If Jay had called Coal to get her out of the city, her brother wasn't coming home anytime soon. But it wasn't even that; it was the caution in the way Coal acted. He hadn't turned on any lights and he stuck to the shadows as if expecting someone to be lingering around the house, watching for her. "They're going to kill me because of him, aren't they?"

"No, baby." He wrapped his arm around her and pulled her tight against his body. "I'm going to protect you, but we've got to go. Do you have everything you want? Anything that's not important we can replace once we get where we're going."

When she nodded, he stepped back, grabbed her duffle bag, and slid it over his shoulder. "Let's go."

She reached back to the dresser, her hand brushing against the butt of the gun when his arm wrapped around her waist and pulled her away. "Wait."

"No." He tugged her toward the door and when she fought him, he pushed her up against the wall. "Can you guarantee me that gun isn't stolen? That it hasn't been used in a crime? Damn it, Syd, I know what Jay's been doing all these years. Tim...your dad...do you want to end up like them? Getting caught with a stolen gun…using the fucking thing…what the hell are you thinking?"

"I'm thinking about staying alive. Just because they've done those things doesn't mean I've done anything wrong."

"Still so naïve." He tucked a strand of her hair behind her ear and shook his head. "The police know you. They know you're connected to Jay. With him out of the picture, they're going to be wondering if you're picking up where he left off. Just like Jay took over from your dad. In the twenty minutes I've been here, I've seen two police cruisers. Do you think that's a coincidence? Every single officer who knows your family is wondering if you're in on it, too. They don't have any proof, but you're the last one left and look where you're living. They'll be watching you."

"But I've never…" She tried to argue but he was right. Three months earlier, Jay was dropping her off at work and they were pulled over for speeding. The car was searched and Jay had drugs on him. He was arrested and she was questioned as if she was guilty by association. That was when she started putting money aside, with the intent on getting the hell out of town. Everyone who knew her family thought she was no good, just like them. "Why come back if you think I'm just like them? Surely you don't want to tarnish your perfect appearance. Mr. Millionaire with it all together, what are you doing here? Slumming?"

The sound of glass shattering stopped him from giving an answer. Instead, he took her hand and pulled her down the stairs, toward the front door. "Stay behind me."

"You don't go toward the noise. That's how everyone ends up dead in a scary movie. Shouldn't we go back upstairs?" Upstairs they'd find them, but there, she had the gun. They could protect themselves. "I can't run forever. Maybe I should just face them."

"Bullshit." At the bottom of the stairs, he glanced out the window next to the door before opening it. "Let's go." He pushed her out the front door, keeping her close to him, as a figure came out of the kitchen.

"Don't fucking move!" the figure in black hollered at them as Coal slammed the front door behind them.

"Move!" He pulled her down the deserted street as bullets rang out behind them. They ran toward the car he pointed to, clicking the universal remote "Get in."

As she climbed into the passenger side, she chanced a look back at the house in time to see a man lumbering off the porch, his weapon pointed in their direction. Coal got in the driver's seat and started the engine. Moments later, gunshots echoed through the stillness of the night. Terror filled her, stealing her breath from her lungs.

"Coal!"

Chapter Two

As Coal sped through his hometown, he didn't have time to take in the changes. He was focused on getting them out of town safely. When he'd arrived in the area, he'd noticed signs of people lingering there, but when no one seemed to be around the house, he couldn't be sure any of the ones he'd seen were those Jay was tangled up with. Thankfully, he'd found the spare key hidden in the same spot they'd kept it in when he was a child, hidden above the backdoor; so he'd let himself in, getting easy access to the house. Without that, it would have taken him longer and they might not have been driving out of the city now. They might be lying dead on the floor in her bedroom or worse.

"Coal…" Sydney's eyes were wide as she stared at him, her body shaking with fear. "I'm…"

"Come here." He pulled her across the bench seat, thankful he'd made arrangements for an older car that would blend into the surroundings of his old city. No middle divider to keep them apart. Taking her hand in his, he brought it to his lap. "It's okay, babe. You're safe now."

"You could have been shot!" Tears sprang to her eyes as she cuddled against his side. "We could have died!"

"But we didn't." Hitting the highway, he pressed the gas pedal harder, needing to put distance between them and the people looking for her.

"You're going to be fine. Try to rest; we're going to be on the road for a while."

"Where are we going?"

"Minnesota."

"What?" She pulled back from him. "You can't be serious. I have work in a few hours."

"You're not going." He shot her a sideways glance and raised an eyebrow at her. "Do you really think you could show up for work and they wouldn't be waiting there for you?"

"I don't know, but my boss—"

"Will find someone to cover for you." He tried not to get angry. She was young, and her life had been suddenly tossed into a blender on high. Everything was changing for her and fuck if he wasn't in the middle of it all. Seeing her again sparked circuits within him that he'd thought were dead. She had drawn his attention back in the days before he'd left town, but she was fucking gorgeous now. "They were willing to kill us tonight. Whatever Jay owes them is bigger than I first thought. Your only chance is to leave town." He wasn't sure how but he'd figure out what mess Jay was in and make sure Syd was safe.

With a huff, she leaned back and stared out the window. "Jay screws up and I'm the one to pay."

"It's going to be okay," he reassured her.

She pulled away from him and brought her legs up onto the seat, hugging them to her chest. Her long blonde hair hid her face from view, making him want to reach over and brush it back, so he could see her. Fighting the urge, he kept his attention on the road and off her. His best friend's baby sister was off-limits. More than that, she was just a kid.

"You always tried to protect me but even you can't keep me sheltered from them. You have to realize that, Coal. They'll find me and you don't

14

need that kind of trouble. It will screw up everything for you, Tanner Cycles, your brothers…there's too much to risk."

"Don't, Syd." He tightened his grip on the steering wheel, when all he wanted to do was reach over and take her hand into his again. "Let me worry about that. Right now, you need to get some sleep. It's going to be okay, I promise. Trust me. Have I ever let you down before?"

"Never." Her voice was whisper quiet but he caught the sadness to it, which made him want to question things further but his phone rang, interrupting him, before he could. He pulled his cell phone from his pocket to see Cayson's name—the next oldest of the Tanner brothers—displayed on the screen. Even if he wanted to, he couldn't ignore the call, so he hit answer and brought the phone to his ear.

"Cay, I thought your partying days were over. What are you still doing up?"

"I'm up because you're neck deep into shit you have no idea about. What the fuck are you doing, bro?" Cay was the no-nonsense brother. While most of the time he only had Cal and Cyrus to bitch at, he'd try to kick Coal's ass into line if he needed it.

"How did you find out?" He wasn't even sure why he asked. It had to be Knuckles. He was the only one who knew Coal had taken off in the middle of the night. When his brothers came to the shop in the morning, they'd have found the note he'd left behind, but it didn't explain anything.

"Yeah. I woke up to the sound of the engines but you were gone before I could get out there. I left a message and he just called me back. He's concerned because you went in alone. Why didn't you let him back you up?"

"This doesn't concern him." Knuckles had experienced brushes with the law in the past, but he'd turned his life around and Coal wasn't going to be the reason their pilot got twisted up in the legal system again. "Now instead of bitching, why don't you go to my office and order the parts that are listed on a printout on my desk?"

"You've got to be joking." Cay huffed. "Have you found her?"

"Yes, and I'm bringing her home."

Cay went silent for a moment, putting Coal on edge, waiting for his brother to say something. "Is that a good idea?"

"It is what it is. You know I'm not going to leave her some place where I can't protect her." He chanced another glimpse at her and found her staring at him, tears glistening in her eyes.

"Do you want me to call Anderson? Maybe he could recommend a criminal lawyer in the area."

"No." The answer was out of his mouth before he had time to think it through. Years of bailing his friend out had worn thin. He was tired of coming to his rescue, pulling him out of whatever muddle he'd gotten into. It wasn't the money. He had more money than he knew what to do with. But Jay wasn't going to learn, and this time had been the final straw. Risking Sydney had burned the last bridge between them. "You want to make yourself useful? Find out what the fuck he's into. It's more than money for drugs. Those fuckers were ready to kill us tonight."

What am I doing? Can I really tangle him up in this? Sydney considered her options and as much as she wanted Coal to ride to her rescue and save her like she was six years old again, it wasn't his responsibility. As of a month ago, she was an adult, and that meant she had to dig herself out of this mess. She wasn't a child, needing someone to come to her rescue. Jay had screwed things up for her worse than he had ever before and she wasn't even sure if he'd make it back out of jail anytime soon. Although she appreciated that Coal had come for her, she couldn't shove him into this situation.

While he was on the phone with Cayson, she tried to put together a plan to convince him she'd be fine on her own. By taking her to Minnesota, Coal wouldn't just be risking himself but his brothers' lives, too. She couldn't allow that. She might have accepted his offer if she hadn't heard Cay's anger through the phone speaker. Family discord because of her would only make the situation more dangerous.

"We're on the road now but we're going to have to stop and get some rest in a few hours, once we're out of the state. I'll send you a text when we stop and once we're back on the road. But if things go well, I'll be back in time. Just make sure Cal gets to work immediately on the bike Knuckles is picking up in Texas. The timeframe is tight. He wants it finished for his son's sixteenth birthday." With that, Coal ended the call and dropped the cell into his lap.

Seeing that as the only opportunity she'd have before her courage fled, she unfolded her legs from in front of her and turned to face him. "While I appreciate your offer to help, I can't—"

"Don't, Syd. Nothing you can say is going to make me pull over and let you out. If you must, think of this as a kidnapping. You're going to Minnesota, whether you like it or not, so let's not fight about it. Okay?"

"Coal, you can't just walk back into my life and demand I listen to you. I'm not a little girl anymore. I have a job and a life. I can't just leave town." She didn't have much of a life. Work and taking care of Jay, but Coal didn't need to know that. Things hadn't turned out as she'd always hoped but at least she hadn't followed her brothers into the family business of drugs.

"I can see you're not a little girl any longer but that doesn't change things. I'm not going to stand by while you get yourself killed because of your fucking brother." He reached across the seat to where she retreated and placed his hand on her leg. "Just relax. We'll fix this and when it's safe, if you want to go home I'll deliver you personally back to that hellhole we just left. If you want to start over anywhere else in the world, I'll help you. You don't need to go back there. What's there for you?"

Instead of answering him, she stared out at the window. What was there for her? She couldn't think of a single thing. Her father had a lengthy prison sentence in front of him, Tim was serving a life sentence, and now Jay would be joining them. With her family behind bars, she was alone. Eighteen and alone. She should be starting college with her friends, her whole life ahead of her. Instead, she was wondering if she even had anything to hope for and dream about. What was her life worth?

Staring out the window, she let her head rest against the back of the seat. Things were so complicated and anger boiled within her. She wanted to scream at Jay for putting her in the middle of the situation; she wanted to push Coal away so he wouldn't get hurt, while at the same time she wanted to let him wrap his arms around her and hold her tightly.

She'd read every article printed about him and Tanner Cycles over and over. Pictures of him filled her memory box. While Jay had put up with her wanting to tag along with him as a child, Coal had been sweet and protective. She'd had a crush on him back then, wanting to be around Jay because Coal would be there. It wasn't until a week before he'd left for Minnesota that she'd learned his true feelings for her. *I'm going to miss you the most, Syd. You're like a little sister to me.*

At thirteen, she'd had her first heartbreak. She didn't want to be a little sister to him—she wanted him to love her like she loved him. With tears streaming down her face, she'd stood on the porch of the same house he'd just rescued her from and watched him hop onto his motorcycle to ride out of her life. Something inside of her had shattered that day. She'd retreated into her room, letting Jay do his own thing without her tagging along. The first time she'd heard from him, she felt anger for him leaving her. She wasn't his responsibility but she'd needed him. He'd been the one good thing in her life. The one thing that kept her sane as everything else around her was falling apart.

The wind ripped through her hair as she ran and tears streamed down her face. She didn't know where she was going; all she knew was she couldn't stay in that house any longer. If one more person wrapped their arms around her and told her they were sorry for her loss, she'd scream. It was all too real, when all she wanted to do was deny it ever happened. The pain and bruises along the right side of her body weren't something she could deny. Every time she looked into the mirror, the gash above her eye wouldn't let her forget.

She dropped to her knees behind the trees that skirted the edge of the playground. "Why...why did you have to leave me? Everything seems so much harder without you here. Daddy's always drinking. Tim...Tim's gone."

"There you are." Coal strolled toward her, his usual t-shirt and jeans were replaced with a suit, and his hair was tugged back into a hair tie. His change in appearance was another reminder of the events that had unfolded in the past week. "Everyone is really worried about you. Why don't you come back to your house with me?"

"He killed them! He took everything from us." She slammed her fists onto the ground, sending the dirt flying through the air. "I hate him! I wish he was dead."

He dropped to his knees beside her and wrapped his arms around her. "I know Syd, I know." Comforting her, he kissed the top of her head, allowing her to bury her face against his chest and let the tears flow freely.

"How can you not hate me?" She clung to him, wishing they could somehow change things.

"Syd! Wake up." Her eyes fluttered opened to find Coal leaning over her, his hands on her shoulders, shaking her. "Syd..."

"What?" Her eyes were heavy and gritty with the weight of the past.

19

"Shit, you scared me." He leaned against the doorframe and she realized they were still on the road.

She looked around, trying to determine where they were, but the nondescript motel in front of her, held little clue of that. The peeling paint and empty lot told her they didn't do much business, or they didn't care. A roadside motel was the last place she expected to find Coal at but something about it seemed to fit him. He never started Tanner Cycles with the goal of making it big, or for the money; he did it because he had a love for motorcycles.

"This car isn't you. Why didn't you bring your bike?"

He let out a lighthearted chuckle and squatted down next to her. "Leave it to you to make me laugh after that."

"After what?"

"Oh, Syd." He reached in and cupped the side of her face. "You were screaming."

"Oh." She looked down at her hands, suddenly embarrassed that her dream had been overheard by him. They had shared that time together but that was the past. "Is that why we've stopped?"

"We stopped to get some sleep. Both of us need it." He held his hand out to her and when she took it, he pulled her up until the front of her body was inches from his. "Are you okay now?"

Even as she nodded, she knew she wasn't. The effects of the dream lingered, making her feel uneasy. She thought that would be the worst part of her life, but after her mother died, things had continued to get worse. Her mother had been the glue that kept the family together, and without her, they seemed to fall apart. She'd give anything to go back to that time, to be young and full of hope.

He raised his eyebrows at her as if he didn't believe her but he didn't question her further. The desire for him to wrap his arms around her again burned within her but he stepped back from her and opened the backseat car door to grab their bags. With their bags in hand, he nodded toward the motel again. "Let's get some rest."

"Where are we?"

"A little more than an hour outside of Indiana. Hell if I know the town's name but I'm sure there's something in the room to enlighten us if you're keen on knowing." Scanning the area, he walked toward the door and slid the old-fashioned key into the lock before holding it open for her. "Inside."

"I thought Jay was the one who got ordered around by guards, not me. When did I become the prisoner?"

"I presume the same time I kidnapped you." A faint smile tugged at the corners of his lips.

She was tempted to fight him but reasoning overcame that urge. He didn't deserve for her to act like that. He'd come to her rescue hours after Jay was taken into custody, whisking her away to safety and risking his own welfare in the process. She didn't want to see him get tied up in this because of her. How could Jay drag him into this after everything that had happened?

Side of the road motels tended to be disgusting but when she stepped into the room she was surprised that it was cleaner than she'd expected. Two full beds with a bedside table between them and a dresser with a television on it—other than that, the room was bare of any decorations. No wall art or welcome pamphlets with local attractions. None of that mattered to her as she plopped down onto the bed and focused on him. "Why did you come?"

"Now, Syd, you know that answer." He set their bags on top of the dresser and turned toward her.

"No, Coal, I don't." Uneasy, she picked at the small hole forming just above the knee of her jeans. "After everything…"

"After nothing. Nothing that happened before matters." He squatted before her and took her hands into his. "You're stressed and you need to rest. Things will look better in the morning."

"You said those same words to me before but things weren't better in the morning. They were worse. Everything was worse." She hated that the tears burned in her eyes again but as much as she tried to blink them away, they seemed to double in intensity. She wanted to go back to a time when things were simpler, a time when her mother was still alive and things were better. "How can you not hate us? Hate me?"

"I could never hate you." He cupped the side of her face with his hand, dragging his thumb gently under her eyes to wipe away the tears that had begun to fall. "Never, Syd. Never."

"You're…" Her voice broke and she had to stop to take a deep breath. "You're the only one who calls me Syd. I've missed it. I've missed you." Every time she spotted him in a magazine or on television, a little piece of her died. One day he had been everything to her and the next day he was gone, leaving behind an empty hole in her chest. *You took my heart with you when you left me.*

Chapter Three

Exhaustion ate at Coal but sleep wouldn't come. Too much weighed on his shoulders. Her words cut like knives into his heart. *How can you not hate me?* Did she think he'd left town because of her? That he blamed her for any of the shit they'd had to go through? Had Jay said something to make her think that? His reasons for leaving town had nothing to do with her and everything to do with the fact he had four younger brothers who looked up to him. They needed someone to step up and keep the family together, to keep them in school, and provide for them—his responsibility, so that's what he did. Leaving Syd had been the hardest part. He'd wanted to toss her into his truck and take her with him, but he couldn't. At the time, she'd been underage.

His cell vibrated with another message from Cal. *Tank's on his way. The car will be swapped by daylight.* He grinned at the phone. Ever reliable, Cay came through for him and would back him on this even if he wasn't sure Coal was making the right decision. His brother had never understood the relationship he had with Syd; hell, how could he when Coal didn't even understand it himself? Not wanting to analyze the relationship right then, he shot a reply. *Thanks. We'll get on the road when Tank arrives.*

The soft light from the television was enough for him to take in the image of Syd lying in the next bed. She hadn't put up much of a fight when he told her they'd share this room, that he wasn't letting her out of his sight, let alone in another room. Separated, they might not be as lucky as they had been back at her house. He didn't believe anyone had followed them but he wasn't willing to take the chance, and if he was honest, he wanted her close.

What did that say about him? She was Jay's little sister. He was supposed to protect her, not think about stripping her out of her clothes and making love to her. About kissing away the sadness in her eyes, and holding her tight against him until the fear stopped consuming her. She had transformed from a teenage girl to a woman in what seemed like a blink of an eye. She'd always had him wrapped around her finger, conning Jay into allowing her to hang out with them.

The age difference should have kept them apart but somehow, they'd managed to overcome that. Maybe it was everything she'd gone through with her family, which made her more mature than some of the girls he knew. While they had always been close, in a friendship sort of way, that had been it. She had been a little sister to him. Now, she brought emotions to life within him he'd never experienced. She called to him in a way a woman called to a man. His dick had been hard for her since his gaze landed on her. The way she clung to him, as if he was all she ever needed, made him want to prove himself to her.

Bro, I hope you know what you're doing. He could have replied to Cay, reassuring him that he was well aware of what he was doing but the one thing he didn't do was lie to his brothers. He'd shield them whenever possible but an outright lie was out of the question. They were all each other had and had stuck together when they were delivered the toughest blow they had ever overcome—the sudden death of their parents.

Readjusting to get comfortable, he leaned back against the headboard only to have the rusted old metal frame creak under his weight. He let his gaze roam from the cell phone still in his hand to her. Concerned the noise

24

had disturbed her after she had finally fallen into a restless sleep only an hour ago, he was pleasantly surprised to find her still in deep slumber.

His thoughts drifted back to the last time she'd been asleep in his company. It seemed like so long ago, a lifetime ago. She was so young, so broken. As for him, he wasn't sure what he was back then. He could barely keep things together, snapping at his brothers for the slightest infractions.

His childhood bedroom was mostly bare, with everything packed in boxes, ready for the move. One of the only things that remained in the room was his bed. Anger and grief ate at him as he stalked toward it, ready to throw his leather jacket onto the mattress, when a fraction of a second before he let go, he realized it was occupied. There in the center of his bed Sydney curled into a tight ball, wearing his t-shirt. Her eyelids fluttered open as if she felt his presence, or maybe she'd heard him coming up the stairs.

"What are you doing here? It's late. You should be home." He dropped his jacket at the foot of the bed.

"Please don't go," she begged, tears running down her face, smearing her makeup. "Or take me with you."

His chest tightened and he dropped onto the bed next to her. She didn't realize how many times he'd thought about that very thing, but it wasn't possible. She was thirteen and he already had enough to take care of with his brothers. Yet, leaving her with her father seemed to be a fate worse than death. Kidnapping a minor would put everything he'd worked for out of reach. He'd lose custody of his own brothers and they were counting on him. He couldn't save everyone, and unfortunately his brothers had to come first. It wasn't a choice he'd made easily but this was the only way to save his family.

Instead of explaining the situation to her, he held his arms out for her until she came to him, and he wrapped them around her, holding her tight against him. "I'm sorry, Syd." One day, he hoped she'd understand. He hoped she'd make it through the hell that her family surrounded her with, and would come out stronger on the other side.

Had she come out stronger on the other side? He wasn't sure. She still seemed so young and innocent. How had she lived through years under her father and still be pure in heart? She knew what her family had done, what they were capable of, and what they were involved in. Yet, she'd stayed strong to the vow she'd made that night and had never followed them down that road of self-destruction. No doubt her commitment had been tested countless times but her will had been stronger than temptation.

While he hadn't made it back to his hometown often—more like he chose not to come back to town—he still kept in touch with her, mostly through occasional emails, but he called her cell phone at least once a year on her birthday.

He dragged his hand through his hair, sending the long strands scattering backwards. She was finally of age. Eighteen as of a few weeks ago. During that call, he'd noticed something different in her voice, but she wouldn't explain. He'd thought it was just the stress from work, but the sadness in her tone had nagged at him until he made the decision to go to her once he could take a break from the business commitments.

Break from business commitments. It hadn't been an excuse at first. At the time, he happened to be in the midst of a big business deal he couldn't just walk away from. But the longer he put it off, the more excuses he found. Going back to face her and possibly finding she had indeed followed in Jay's footsteps would have killed something within him. Distance hadn't hidden from him that Jay was getting deeper involved with the life of crime he had chosen and it would have been only a matter of time before he was in too deep. Had that already happened or would he be able to save her from the mess her brother had left her neck deep in?

"Your brows are knitted together in deep thought." She propped up onto her elbow and watched him.

"You're supposed to be sleeping. Jay would be pissed if he thought I wasn't taking care of you."

"Jay has enough of his own problems." She pushed down the blanket and sat up. "You're worried. Did Cay find something? Do you think someone followed us? Is that why you haven't slept?" She threw the questions at him without giving him a chance to answer any of them.

"Everything is fine."

"Don't lie to me." She shot off the bed and moved toward the bathroom before turning back to him. "I'm not a child anymore. I don't need you sheltering me from what's happening. If they're tailing us, I have a right to know."

"Fuck, Syd." He hopped off the bed and stalked toward her. She took a step back. That didn't sit well with him. The fear in her eyes sent pains through his chest. What had happened that she was afraid of him? For her to back away from him after all the years they had spent together was worse than when he had been shot by her shithead brother. If anyone laid a hand on her, there wasn't a doubt in his mind that he'd kill them. Yet, as much as he wanted to close the distance between them, he stopped himself and dropped his hands to his sides. "Oh baby, what happened to you?"

"Noth—"

"Now who's lying?" Unable to resist this time, he went to her when the fear in her eyes was taken over by sorrow. "Talk to me, baby."

"Like you're talking to me." She shook her head. "Just forget it."

"No." He wrapped his hand around her wrist, stopping her before she could pull away from him. "Truth."

"I thought we promised to always be truthful to each other?"

"You're right. Come here." Holding her wrists, he pulled her away from the wall to sit on his bed. He sat down next to her then took her hand in his, interlocking their fingers. The simple act felt right, but it also made him want something more, something he couldn't have. "We learned more about the situation Jay is involved with."

"How bad is it?"

"Bad." He squeezed her hand. "Jay was transporting meth across state lines. This is his third felony drug charge, and with the laws in Pennsylvania, you and I both know they're going to hit him hard for that, but there's more. He had a gun on him when they arrested him. That's bad enough since he's a felon but…"

She turned to look at him when he stopped. "What?"

His anger at Jay raged within him. If he ever got his hands on that bastard, he wasn't sure if he'd be able to allow his old friend to walk away from the encounter. To have to tell Syd that her brother might be responsible for murder was enough to break the resolve within him and have him heading back to Pittsburgh to have a chat with his old buddy. Jay was all Syd had left and the fact that he'd chosen a life of crime over keeping her safe enraged Coal. She deserved better than that. How did a family of lawbreakers end up with such a perfect daughter?

"Coal…" Her voice was hesitant as if she was afraid of what he'd say.

"The gun he had on him has been linked to another crime." With his thumb, he caressed the back of her hand and for the first time since they'd sat down on the bed, he met her gaze. "Syd, Jay may be facing murder charges."

"Murder!" She shook her head. "He wouldn't…"

The urge to comfort her, to tell her things would be fine and that Jay couldn't have had anything to do with it, lingered within him, but he kept his mouth shut. She deserved better than that. He couldn't say Jay hadn't pulled the trigger knowing that his friend was entirely capable of doing just that. He wouldn't lie to her by telling her it would be fine and Jay wouldn't be in prison for murder because the way the evidence was mounting, it was entirely possible. From what Cay gathered, the cops had already suspected him of the murder but they hadn't had enough evidence to charge him. Now, with the gun, it seemed to seal the case with a giant red bow.

Sydney couldn't stop the tears from rolling down her face. Coal wrapped his arm around her shoulders, holding her tight against him, and offering her what comfort he could. She was too lost to take in the words he whispered in her ear. She was all too aware of Jay's life of crime—but murder? She didn't want to believe it but the image of him coming home with blood on his clothes flashed before her eyes.

Exhausted, she sat in the dark living room, waiting. Jay promised he'd be home early, that they could have dinner together. It was her eighteenth birthday and while Jay had offered to throw her a party or take her out to dinner, she'd opted for a quiet meal at home with just the two of them. A party wouldn't have been for her. The only people who would have shown up were Jay's friends. The others from school had kept their distance since—

The door opened and Jay staggered in. She was surprised that he was drunk, but it hurt more that he hadn't remembered what day it was. He barely shut the door behind him when she questioned him. "Where have you been?" She flicked on the lamp beside the sofa, revealing her presence. With the light casting a warm glow over the shabby living room, she could see the state he was in, the blood smeared across his shirt, his hands covered in blood. "Shit, Jay! What happened to you? Are you hurt?"

"It's…it's not…mine," he stuttered, and swayed on his feet.

"Whose—" He held up his hand, stopping her before she could finish the question, and it might have been for the best. She didn't want to know whose blood it was or what he had done.

"Don't stand there and look so innocent." He staggered farther into the room, barely making it to the first chair before collapsing. "You're part of this family and the

same rage that boils within me runs inside of you. I've protected you this long, as I promised Dad I would, but it's time you stepped into the family business."

"Never." She shook her head violently enough to hear her neck crack. "I've never wanted anything to do with that shit. I wish you'd get out. I don't want you to end up in prison like Dad and Tim"

"I'm not as stupid as them. I'll leave the country before the police can lock me in a cage for the rest of my life." Dragging a whiskey bottle out of the front pocket of his jacket, he used his other hand to draw attention to the blood he was covered in. "What do you think this is from? I'll tell you I didn't get this much blood on me from shaving."

"Don't, Jay, I don't want to know."

"Well, know this…" He pushed up out of the chair and came to stand close to her. The stench of alcohol and blood clung to him, making her sick from the very smell. "If you're not part of the business, you're expendable. I won't risk my life any longer for some bitch who thinks she's too good for her family."

"Syd…" The softness in Coal's voice as he called her name forced the demons from her past away. "It's going to be okay."

"My family…" She tipped her head to look at him and realized that, while she'd been lost in her thoughts, he had gotten her to move deeper onto the bed. They now leaned against the headboard, his arm tightly around her, holding her against the length of his body. The spare blanket he had pulled out from the dresser drawer earlier was now draped over her. The sweetness of his actions filled her chest with a lightness that hadn't been there before. Coal was a caring and attentive man. How could she drag him down with her family?

"What, baby?" He caressed his finger along the curve of her cheek. "What about them?"

"Murderers…they're murderers." She let out a deep breath, relieved to finally say it aloud. If there was one person who wouldn't judge her, it would be Coal. He knew what they were capable of and still, he'd come for her. "My father sold teenagers drugs from a batch that he knew was laced. Two died because he didn't care about anything other than making money. Tim—"

"Don't, Syd. Just leave it in the past."

She nodded, giving in to him because it wasn't something she wanted to discuss, either. "Now Jay..."

"Just because he had the gun in his possession doesn't mean he's guilty."

"I wish I could believe that but I know. He all but told me the truth the night he came home covered in blood. That was two weeks ago. I had until the end of the month to join him in the family business or move out. He was tired of taking care of me."

"What were you going to do?" There was a hesitation in his voice, as if he was worried he wouldn't like the answer.

"I didn't know." She sat up, leaning out of his embrace, letting the blanket pool at her waist. "I mean, I wasn't going to join Jay but I couldn't afford to live on my own, either. I'm not...I mean I wasn't getting enough hours at the shop to afford my own apartment. I thought about finding a roommate but even that would have been tough. I tried finding another job but everyone knows what my family brings with it and no one was willing to take a chance on me. I only got the job at the candy shop because it's Vicky's grandfather's place. He's getting old and can't work the long hours, and Vicky started college so she's unavailable during the day. In the end, I only get a handful of hours and it would be cheaper for them to cut back on the shop hours than have me working for them. So who knows how long until I'm out of a job? Anyway, that's a moot point now..."

It dawned on her that when she wouldn't show up for work in a few hours, she'd lose her job. It wouldn't matter that Vicky had helped get her the job. Mr. Reilly didn't care for her and he would see this as a way to finally get rid of her. He'd see it as proof that she was just like the rest of her family—good for nothing trash. If she made it back to Pittsburgh, she'd have nothing to go back to. Her childhood home was unsafe and now, she'd be unemployed.

"I guess it doesn't matter. I'm sure I can't talk you into taking me home now so I can make it to work on time. Therefore, I'm out of work." She hated the defeat that lingered in her words. She wanted to be strong, to hold it together, and have faith that Jay would get out of the charges and come home again. Even trying to muster everything within her, she couldn't. Every member of her family was behind bars and if she wanted to stay alive, she'd have to trust Coal. When this was over, she'd find a way to pay him back for everything he was risking to help her. She turned back to him, not really expecting an answer but wishing he'd say something.

"Out of the question. You're coming home to Minnesota with me and we'll figure out what to do next. Cal's monitoring the situation and will let us know if official murder charges have been filed. He's also looking into whatever debt Jay might have that has put a bounty on your head. Until then, you're just going to have to put up with me."

"That's such a hardship," she joked. She'd put up with him every day of her life if she could. When he moved, he'd left her with an ache in her chest that never went away. Their sporadic phone calls and rare visits weren't enough, the only thing that helped ease the loneliness were the emails they exchanged. He had been her best friend, her first crush, and the man who'd stolen her heart, all rolled into one. Now he was her knight in shining armor.

"Girl, you have no idea what you're getting into." He pulled her back against his chest and snuggled tight against her. "We need to get some rest."

32

"I should go back to my own bed," she whispered even as she enjoyed the feeling of his warmth along her skin and the way his breath teased along the curve of her shoulder.

"I'd rather you stay right here." He squeezed her tighter with the arm he'd draped over her waist, letting her know she wasn't going anywhere.

With anyone else that would have scared her and she'd have fought to get away from them, but with Coal, things were different. She was safe with him and in his arms was where she'd wanted to be for a long time. Rather than fight, she relaxed into his embrace and let her eyes drift shut. Sleep neared, lowering her guard, and she voiced the one question she was terrified to hear the answer to. "What if I'm just like them? Could my temper one day turn into a murderous rage?"

"No, Syd, you don't have that inside of you. You're like your mom. Sweet, innocent, and one of a kind. There's not a drop of that evil in you." He pressed his lips to her temple. "Trust me."

Wanting to believe him, she clung to him. If he stayed next to her when she fell asleep, she'd wake up with him. Maybe she couldn't wish it all away but she could hope to wake up safe in his embrace. Nothing could touch her as long as Coal was there. *My savior...*

Chapter Four

The night had been rough for Coal before Sydney woke up but after, things got worse. How did he convince her she could never do the things her brothers and father had done? She was pure and full of light; the darkness tainting the rest of her family couldn't tarnish her. The plan had been for him to keep his distance from her. That was why, even though they were sharing a room, they had separate beds. She was beautiful and had she been anyone else, he wouldn't deny he wanted her—but she was Syd. As a stand-in big brother, it was his job to protect her. She was off limits, but the rod in his jeans hadn't gotten the message.

He woke up to a message from Cay letting him know that the car had been swapped and Tank was outside waiting for them. They should get on the road, but the joy of having her in his arms, looking so peaceful in her sleep, stopped him from waking her. He wanted to lean down and press his lips to hers, to kiss her gently until she woke, and then take things further. She brought to life a part of him he'd never thought he had. Women had come and gone in his life over the years, but never once had he been affected by any of them as he was with her.

"Fucking beautiful," he whispered more to himself than anyone else as he teased his fingers gently along the curve of her hip bone. "And so fucking young."

"Age is only a number." Her voice was thick with sleep as her eyes flutter open.

"Only old people say that when they want to feel younger." He tucked a strand of her hair behind her ears and forced himself to pull away from her before he did something they'd both regret.

"Don't, Coal." She sat up and grabbed hold of his hand before he could slip off the bed. Her long blonde hair tumbled down around her shoulders, wild and free, and her dark brown eyes stared at him with pain filling them. "Don't push me away. Don't shut me out because you think I'm too young."

"We need to hit the road." He rose off the bed and her hand dropped away from his. "Shower if you want. We'll get breakfast on the road." Moving toward the door, he grabbed his leather jacket and slipped it on.

"Where are you going?"

"I'll be just outside the door talking to Tank. When you're ready, just open the door." He forced himself to look away from her, when all he wanted to do was go back over to the bed and pull her into his arms. The urge to kiss her was almost overpowering. Aware she didn't know Tank but unable to take the time to explain, he opened the door and strolled out. It was an asshole move but better than going back over to the bed and kissing her senseless.

If he managed to keep his dick in his pants long enough to see her out of danger, it would be a miracle. The thought of fucking her made his stomach tight. His youngest brothers were near her age; they should be the ones pursuing her, not him—but the idea of either Cain or Cyrus being interested in her made him want to knock their teeth in.

At least he hoped he wouldn't have to worry about Cain taking interest in her, because if things went well, he wouldn't even know she was there. Cain had a small cabin farther in on their property; unable to handle being around others, he kept to himself. He had his problems but the brothers stuck together and they'd protect Cain with their lives if they had to.

Cyrus, on the other hand, was another story. He'd turned eighteen six months earlier, so he was eager to prove himself and wanted to take more responsibilities around the shop. Hopefully, that would be enough motivation for him to stay away from Syd; otherwise, Coal would have to take things a bit further. He wouldn't stand around and watch his brother flirt with his girl.

Fuck, I did not just think of Syd as my girl. His head was so screwed up, he wasn't even sure a shrink would make sense of it. Syd wasn't his but damn if he didn't want her.

"Hey, you ready to roll out?" Tank leaned against the front of the SUV that Coal had requested be the replacement vehicle.

"Almost. She's getting ready now." He dragged his hand through his hair and looked over the black SUV. They still had hours left on their journey. There was no reason why they couldn't ride in something nicer than that piece of shit he'd picked her up in. This still wasn't his normal ride but it would work for the time being. Tank's bike was parked next to it, reminding Coal he'd be alone with Syd for the rest of the trip. It was unlikely that she'd sleep, but he hoped they could keep the conversation on safe topics. Anything to keep his mind off the fantasy of pushing her down on the bed and fucking her until she screamed his name. "Thanks for coming, Tank."

"Anytime, man." Tank straightened up so he was no longer leaning against the SUV. "There's a sandwich shop around the corner. They have great breakfast sandwiches. I'm going to grab one. Want one?"

"Sure, and grab one for her." He went to pull his wallet out of his pocket but Tank shook his head, stopping him.

Tank had just kind of shown up in the Tanner brothers' lives and stuck around. He wasn't just considered a good friend—he was family. In order to fund his love for traveling, he'd put time in at the shop with the brothers, doing a little bit of this and that, but his strength was in security. As a former Army Ranger, he still came in handy occasionally.

"Who's he?" Syd stood in the doorway, drawing Coal's thoughts back to the present.

"A good friend. You ready?" His gaze traveled over her body, disappointed that her long, sexy legs were now encased in jeans. He wanted nothing more than to coax her back into that hotel room and pull those jeans off with his teeth. His dick hardened enough that he was left with no choice but to readjust his clothing.

"I could help you with that if you'd let me." She wiggled her eyebrows at him. "Come on, handsome. We've got some time before he gets back."

"No." He stepped toward her, but when she didn't move out of the doorway, he fought the urge to press her up against the doorframe and show her she was playing with fire. "Syd—"

"What's wrong with me?" She glanced down at his crotch before her gaze travel back up to meet his. "It's obvious that you're turned on, so why won't you touch me? Are you repulsed by me? Or is it because you know what my family has done and you don't want to get involved with someone who could possibly be as unstable as they are?"

He grabbed hold of her hand and forced it against his chest before sliding it down toward his aching dick. "Does this look like I'm repulsed by you?" He guided her hand over the length of him, only the fabric of his jeans and boxers between them, the simple caresses making him harder by the second. "Baby, you have no idea what you do to me."

"Then why reject me when all I want to do is ease your suffering?" She cupped his dick in her hand, rubbing down the length of it. "Why not let me take care of this?"

"No." He forced himself to take a step back. Having a rock hard cock was better than using her in that way. She deserved better than that from any man, but she most certainly deserved better than that from him.

"So then it comes back to my family history." This time it wasn't a question; she was simply stating a fact as she saw it.

"You know that's not it. You're not unstable. This…this is on me. Not you." It was her fucking age. She was too young for him. A baby, just starting out, and he had no right to her. Jay trusted him with her—fuck, her own mother had asked him to watch out for her. This would be going against everything her mother had wanted for her.

"Bullshit." Shaking her head, she reached down and grabbed her duffle bag that he hadn't noticed by her feet. "I should respect the fact that you don't want to get involved with someone like me."

That comment was all it took for him to push her back against the door, his mouth on hers in a frenzied, desire filled moment. The sweet, fruity taste of her lip gloss should have been enough to remind him why he needed to stop; instead, it only encouraged him more. Using his tongue, he urged her mouth to open, to let him in. Their tongues danced together as she dropped the duffle bag and wrapped her arms around his neck, pulling him closer. He rubbed against her, making sure she felt how hard she had made him. She did this to him—no one else. There was no doubt about it; she would be his undoing.

A throat cleared from behind them and he didn't have to look to know it was Tank. With one final kiss, he forced himself to stop. He didn't step back from her; instead, he lowered his head to the curve of her shoulder. "Don't doubt for one second I want you."

"I hate to interrupt but we should be going. There's a lot of ground to cover."

He stepped back, grabbed the bag at their feet, and turned to the other man. "Tank, this is Syd. Syd, meet Tank."

"I brought breakfast." Tank held up a bag and two coffees as if offering them in peace. "I wasn't sure if you like coffee or prefer something else. The clerk tossed some flavored creamers into the bag for you just in case."

"Thank you." She stepped past Coal to take one of the coffees and the bag. "I'm starving."

"Get in the SUV and eat. I'll grab the bags. And Tank, I should have told you to get the whole box of creamers. She takes a little coffee with her cream." Knowing she was in safe hands, he turned to shoot Cay a text message, letting him know they were on the road.

"I can ride over and get some more before we hit the road," Tank offered as Syd opened the brown bag in search of the creamers.

"Coal's joking. Not everyone likes their coffee black as sin, like he does. There are plenty. Even if there weren't enough I wouldn't turn this down. Coffee is coffee and I need the caffeine today."

Coal shook his head. He'd seen her drink creamer straight out of the container and he wouldn't be one bit surprised if the only reason she drank coffee was for an excuse to have creamer. He grabbed his bag off the dresser and shoved his phone back into his pocket before strolling out of the room. Tonight they'd be back at his place. The sleeping situation was something that would need to be worked out, but there wasn't a chance in hell he'd let her out of his sight until things were taken care of with the thugs that were after her. Temptation at its finest would be in his bed by the day's end. The question was, would he be able to keep his hands off her?

During the uneventful drive, Sydney saw sparks of the young man who'd left her years ago, carefree and full of life—until that tragic day when everything had changed. Less than a month later, she'd lost him and everything they had together. That was when she'd realized how quickly her world was falling apart. Tim was facing charges that would put him behind bars for life, if not on death row. Now they were pretty much the same since the governor had put a halt on all executions but during his trial, execution had still been a real possibility. Jay and her father had been wrapped up in their own grief, leaving her on her own.

Thirteen years old and no one cared if she even came home at night. She'd taken over her mother's role in the house, cooking and cleaning. Even if there were no longer family dinners, she always made sure there was food in the refrigerator for when Jay and Dad decided to eat. She'd set her alarm for four in the morning to make sure her father was up for work and to make him breakfast. Jay used to call her 'little wifey' and while that bothered her, she knew that if she didn't do all the things she did, nothing would get done. It wasn't long after her mother's death that her father had lost his job. By the time she was sixteen, he was looking at a prison term that compared to Tim's, leaving her alone with only Jay.

"Now who's lost in thought?"

She blinked and realized Coal wasn't sitting next to her any longer, but standing next to her with her car door open and their bags in his hand. "We're here?" She looked past him to what appeared to be an older warehouse. Might have been three stories, but the old brick building could have extra high ceiling, giving that illusion. There was nothing surrounding it but open space and trees—not what she expected at all.

41

"Yeah." He tipped his head toward the line of trees where the taillights of Tank's motorcycle were beginning to fade. "Cay, Cal, and Cyrus share the house on the other side of the landing strip. Tank will spend the night there."

She tried to take in the house that he pointed at but it was too dark. All she could make out was that it had two stories, and only because the lights on both floors were on. "What about Cain? He's not here?"

"His place is farther back in the trees. But Syd, I want you to stay away from him. Do you understand me?"

"Yes." Cain had always been a little different from his brothers, but something had happened to him. There were rumors that circulated but she'd never believed any of them. Maybe because she didn't want to think that her brother was to blame for yet another thing. Being young should have meant she was sheltered from all the horrors that had happened, but this wasn't the case. Her father had sat her down and told her what had transpired. What he'd left out, the children at school made sure she knew.

Not wanting to focus on the past, she looked up at Coal's dark brown eyes, willing herself to get lost in them and forget about everything else. "What about me? Where are you going to put me since you won't let me go home?"

"You are coming home with me." He took her hand and gently tugged her away from the SUV. "I live above the shop."

"Why would I think any different? You're a workaholic and being close allows you to put in extra hours without having to go anywhere but upstairs when you're ready to crash." She pushed the passenger door shut with her other hand so she didn't have to let go of his.

"Maybe, but also because I like it here." His steps quickened. "You'll see what I mean."

They stepped into the shop, into an open space with various motorcycles in different stages of completion. She wanted to take her time, to see the different areas that had been set up, but Coal didn't give her time to take it all in. He continued toward the staircase that stood off against the far wall, forcing her to follow. The black wrought iron railing had curves and detail to it that surprised her, and mixed nicely with the dark wood of the stairs.

At the top they reached a large office. The glass windows allowed the person inside to look down at the shop below. Stepping into the room, she immediately knew it was Coal's workspace. Not only did the simple décor with the large, cluttered desk scream his name, but the lingering scent of his cologne hung in the air. This was his office, no doubt, but it felt personal, like she was invading his space. As she looked around, Coal placed his bag on the sofa along the wall and pulled out his laptop.

"Are you seriously about to work? We've been on the road all day. You have to be exhausted." Even as she questioned him, she realized he most likely was behind because of having to make the trip to Pennsylvania to come to her rescue. They couldn't have flown back because they couldn't risk anyone seeing her leave and follow them—which meant the trip had been longer with them driving.

"Worried about me?" He raised his eyebrow at her in question. "No, I'm just putting this down here so I'm not tempted to work tonight." He placed the laptop on the desk, careful not to knock over the stacks of papers that cluttered the surface.

She looked at the papers, and certain things caught her attention. It appeared most of it was accounting, things that needed added into the books, parts ordered, requests for custom bikes or jobs. How did he keep up with all of that himself? "It looks like you need help."

"You have no idea."

"Don't you have an assistant?"

"No." Without further explanation, he grabbed the bags and nodded toward another staircase. "Ready?"

Unlike the other stairs, this was closed off from view but just as wide. The wrought iron didn't have as much of a role here, being simply a twisted handrail that ran along the wall. The stairs were the same dark wood as before and with every step she climbed, she had a nagging feeling she was venturing into a place few had the privilege to enter. It should have made her feel special, but the weight of knowing she wouldn't have been here if Jay hadn't been arrested weighed on her. She didn't want to be an obligation; she wanted to be there because he wanted her with him. For the first time since her mother passed away, she wanted to feel wanted.

"I shouldn't be here."

At the top of the stairs, Coal dropped the bags and came back to where she'd stopped. He sat down two steps above her so they were eye level with each other. He took her hand into his, pulling them against his chest. "Let's not start that again."

"It's the truth. You've done too much for me, risked too much. I can never repay you for this. Jay had no right to even ask this of you." Her thoughts ran together. "I could kill him for putting you in this position."

"Baby, I want you here." He rubbed his thumb along the curve of her knuckles. "I know everything looks dismal right now but we're going to fix this. Cal's working on making contact with those who are after you. We'll see what we can do to clear up the situation."

"They'll want their drugs or their money and I have neither."

"Then we'll pay them."

He stated it like it was so simple. Money might not be anything to him but every dollar she ever had she'd worked hard for. She'd fought to keep it from her family, hiding it away in different spots, hoping they'd never find it. For her, paying them wasn't simple. She couldn't allow him to do that for her. It was too much and would drop him dead center into the mix. "No."

"Enlighten me on your reasoning."

"Are you serious?" Her voice rose as she looked at him. Silently, he waited for her to answer, making her shake her head. "I don't have the money for that and I can't let you do that. It would drop you and your family right into it once they find a connection. Drug dealers and who knows what else Jay is involved with. They would jeopardize your business, your livelihood, and your family."

"Don't worry." He reached up and cupped the side of her face. "Nothing's going to happen to me. Cal's working on it, but we're using a third party. Nothing will be traced back to us. Not because I'm worried about the police or some drug dealer. They'll never find out we're the ones taking care of it, or that you're here. You'll be protected. I promise."

"Why are you doing all of this?" She wanted to believe that everything would be okay but the fear she had been living with most of her life seemed to become suddenly overwhelming. She wasn't sure how to deal with it any longer.

"For you, Syd." Grabbing the back of her head, he brought her down to the step in front of him so she was kneeling between his legs and their faces were so close, she could feel his breath on her cheek. "You deserve the world. Everything you've ever wanted should be yours for the taking."

"If only life worked like that."

"Come on." He stood and took her hand in his. "Let's get you settled and if you want to watch a movie or something, I'll make popcorn."

"Movie night, just like old times." There were aspects from the relationship they had before—especially the ease of everything—that she wanted back. While on the other hand, she wanted to take things to another level. The man she'd wanted for as long as she could remember stood before her and she had the opportunity to see where things went. Maybe they wouldn't go anywhere. Maybe he was dating someone, even if she hadn't heard about it through the gossip magazines or Internet. Either way, she had to try. He said she deserved anything she wanted. Well, she wanted him.

# Chapter Five

The next morning, Sydney stood at the loft railing, looking out over his sanctuary. The space was amazing. Modern and clean, yet welcoming and lived in. It was him, down to the simplest aspects. The large living area down below had a huge dark brown sectional that almost looked like leather, but was soft and welcoming. There was enough seating room for all his brothers to sprawl out and probably half a dozen more people. The television dominated the wall but below it, the fireplace proved just as much of an eye catcher.

The only surprising part of the entertaining space was the kitchen. The Coal she knew could do the basics when it came to cooking, but the kitchen here was fit for a chef. The large prep countertop would make anyone envious with the bar stools lining the opposite side. The bar was made of concrete, but it somehow fit the place. The exposed beams and ductwork were reminders that this had at one time been a warehouse and he had turned it into a home.

The loft overlooked the whole space and fit his personal style and requirements. The king size bed stood against the stone wall, with no headboard or bedframe to distract the eye from the natural stone, taken from the creek that ran through the property. The night before, prior to crawling into the bed, she'd ran her fingers over the smooth walls and he had explained that they had been worn thin by the water cascading over them for years. The charcoal comforter was heavy and plush, inviting her to curl up under it.

This was his personal space but he had allowed her to spend the night there while he had been a gentleman and slept on the sofa. Thinking of him, her gaze traveled to where he still lay asleep. Her heart skipped a beat as she wished she was waking up in his arms again. As if feeling her gaze on him, his eyes fluttered open. Embarrassed, she spun away to look around the room again. A picture next to the bed caught her attention. There were other photographs around the room, most of them on the long ebony dresser that lined the wall next to the walk-in closet. She had been too tired to take them in the previous night and had crawled into bed almost immediately to sleep. This picture frame was the only one on the nightstand, piquing her attention.

She walked across the room and picked it up. The image had her dropping onto the bed.

It was a week before Halloween and the chillness in the air sent a shiver through her but she stood waiting on her front porch in her prettiest dress, her hair pulled back in a French braid her mother had done for her that morning. He'd come—he always came; she just had to be patient.

"What's so special about today, sweetie?" her mother asked, carrying two glasses of her homemade iced tea and chocolate chip cookies out onto the porch.

"Coal will be here soon. Jay's sick but Coal promised he'd come to take me to the park. It's just going to be the two of us."

"Sweetie…" Her mother sat the tray down and came to kneel in front of her. "Coal might be busy. He's a big boy, just like Jay. I can take you to the park in a bit."

"No!" She slammed her little foot down, making the wood under her feet groan. "He promised!"

"Would I ever let you down?" Coal came around the side of the house, a grin stretched across his face. "Get Jay and we'll go."

"Coal!" she screamed, running down the stairs into his arms. "You came! I knew you would."

"I'm afraid Jay's sick. He's not able to go today," her mother explained, rising off her knees. "I was trying to explain that to Sydney just now."

"Mrs. Manor, if you're fine with it, I'd still like to keep my promise and take her to the park."

Her mother's eyebrow rose in question at his statement. "I'm sure you have better things to do than watch her."

"Mommy, please?"

"I have the afternoon off and nothing else planned." He glanced down at her then back up at her mother. "I'd hate to disappoint her and I'm sure you have your hands full with both Jay and Tim sick. We'd just be down the street at the park."

Relenting, her mother nodded. "Okay, but Sydney I want you to go inside and get your sweater."

Without hesitation, she ran back inside the house. When she came out, she found her mother standing closer to Coal, her voice hushed as they finished their conversation. Not knowing what they were discussing, she ran back to Coal, the excitement of spending the afternoon with him at the park coursing through her.

"You know how much she means to me."

"Yes, Mrs. Manor. You have my word." He took her hand, squeezing it softly.

"Thank you, Coal." She gave him a quick smile before looking down at Sydney. "Now you behave yourself and when he says it's time to come home, I want you to listen. None of that 'just five more minutes' backtalk you give me. Understand?"

"Yes, Mom."

"Go on. I'll save your iced tea and cookies for when you return."

Moments later, they were strolling down the block, heading toward the park, her hand in his. Everything seemed so perfect. Jay wasn't with them to ruin the afternoon with his attitude. *She wasn't happy about what had happened to him but having the afternoon alone with Coal held too much excitement for her to worry about her brother.*

"I thought you'd come down." Coal stood at the top of the stairs, a pair of pajama pants slung low on his hips and his chest bare. "What do you have there?"

If it's possible, I want you more now than I did that day. Instead of answering, she held out the picture to him and when his gaze landed on it, his lips curled up into a smile but the lightness of it didn't quiet reach his eyes. "I didn't know she'd taken a shot of it." Heat filled her cheeks as she realized her mother had taken a picture forever capturing her most embarrassing moment.

"You remember." More of a statement than a question, but she nodded.

"I remember." Images of that day continued to float through her mind, wrapping her up and transporting her back to an innocent time.

Everything about the afternoon at the park was perfect and by the time they made it back to the house for tea and cookies, she knew that it was now or never. Plating the cookies, she glanced up at him. "Marry me, Coal?"

"Excuse me." He choked on his iced tea, coughing as he tried to clear his airway.

"Marry me. I love you. Mommy said one day I'd find a husband, one who would cherish me. Instead..." She stopped, not willing to discuss what had happened behind closed doors. She placed her hand over his, her little hand so small in his larger one. "You gave me the courage to come down from the tree. I want you in my life. Mommy says you can't be my brother like Jay and Tim, so I've decided I want to marry you. Then you can always be here."

"Sweetie..." He adjusted uneasily in his chair. "You're too young to make that decision. You have so much growing to do yet. You don't know who you want to spend the rest of your life with yet."

"I know I want you."

"And I'll always be there for you. I'm like a big brother but the best part is I don't have to report to your mom and dad. You can tell me anything you want without risking getting in trouble. We can go to the park just like today, and have fun whenever we want, without the commitment of marriage." He took her hand into his and smiled at her. *"One day when you're older you'll realize that I'm not the man you want. I'm too old."*

"What if I still want you?"

He was silent for a moment, as if unsure what to say. "Then we'll discuss it when the time comes. No matter what, Syd, you'll always be my special girl."

"I guess my girl has something for older men," her mother joked, coming near them with a fresh pitcher of tea.

"You saved me from falling to my death and I became infatuated with you. You must have hated me." She couldn't even look up at him. Was she doing that again? No, she'd never stopped wanting him. He had been the one good thing in her life.

"You were only five feet off the ground. You weren't going to die." He sat down next to her on the bed, close enough that their shoulders brushed against each other. "You were so scared of heights. I still don't know why you even climbed that tree."

"I was even more scared of spiders." She turned her head to look at him. "Billy Fuller had one and backed me up against the tree, threatening to let it loose on me. The only way I could get away from him was up the tree."

"Ah, Billy. I remember that little punk." He reached over and took her hand. "I could never hate you and your infatuation was adorable."

"Adorable, but you wouldn't marry me," she teased. "I couldn't have been that cute."

"You were cute then but you're gorgeous now."

"You told me that when I was older I would realize you were wrong for me." She twisted so that she could look at him. "You were wrong. I still want you, Coal Tanner."

"Fuck, baby, don't say that." He turned to face her.

"Kiss me." She reached up and touched his cheek, the five o'clock shade tickling along her fingers. "Please, Coal."

"This is wrong. I'm supposed to be your protector." Even as he argued against it, he leaned into her and claimed her lips.

The soft peck of a kiss turned hot and full of passion the moment her mouth opened, allowing him access. He wrapped his hand around the back of her head and slid his tongue into her mouth, forcing a moan from deep within her. She wanted him like nothing she'd ever wanted before. He was everything that she would ever need. She yearned to scoot closer to him on the bed, to feel his body against hers, but she resisted the urge out of fear that it would break the spell and he would come back to his senses.

As if reading her mind, he reached out, wrapped his arm around her waist, and tugged her against him. With one last kiss on her lips, he tipped his head and kissed along her neck. His teeth scrapped over her skin, while he fisted her hair, just enough for her to know he was in control. His warm breath brushed along her neck, sending goosebumps over her skin. Unable to control herself any longer she reached over to run her fingers along his chest, needing to feel the contours of his muscles under her fingers.

"Fuck!" He pulled back from her and shot off the bed before she had a chance to stop him.

"Coal." Her chest tightened with the sudden change in him.

"What the fuck am I doing?" He shook his head, sending his shoulder length dark brown locks into his face. "You're a child, I'm supposed to protect you, not force myself on you."

"I'm eighteen and you're not forcing yourself on me." Jay thought she was old enough to step up and help him run drugs and who knows what else, while Coal could only see her as a child. This was screwed up on a number of levels. The one person she wanted to see her as a woman was rejecting her.

"Eighteen…" He leaned against the dresser, his arms crossed over his wide chest, and watched her. "I know. You don't know what you want. You've just begun to live. I remember what I was like at eighteen."

"Me too." She met his gaze, willing to challenge him if he wanted to go down this road. "You were working full time and going to school at night. When you weren't trying to keep Jay out of trouble, you were helping your mother raise your brothers, or doing things for me. You knew what mattered and had a plan to get out of the city. So don't you dare stand there and tell me I don't know what I want."

"Syd—"

"I'm a big girl, Coal. I've been on my own since you left. My father was too drunk to give a shit about any of us. Jay was moving into the shit Tim left in his wake and training some young kid to continue running the drugs on the street. With Tim behind bars, Jay thought he was the one running the show, the king of the streets. When Dad got that huge shipment of cocaine, it pissed off Jay but when things went down…"

"He was thankful that it was your father going to prison instead of him," he supplied when her words died off. "I know. He called me, relieved that he hadn't taken that shipment. That was the first time he'd ever admitted to dealing drugs, at least to me. Before that, he only admitted to being a hired hand when needed. He said he'd fuck up anyone who needed it, but he wasn't a hired hitman."

"That didn't last long." She leaned forward, dragging her hand through her hair, and looked at him.

"Whatever Jay has done, that isn't your burden to carry."

"I can't help but wonder, how many people did my father kill with that batch of drugs that he knew was laced? He's in prison for the death of two teenagers, but how many more did the police not have enough evidence to charge him with? Tim killed three people with his drunk driving accident. All the blood that my family has spilled and it feels like it's all resting on my shoulders. That somehow I have to be better than everyone else so I can make up for all the evil they brought into this world." What scared her the most was that one day maybe she'd snap and would be just as evil as her family.

"Syd..." He came to squat in front of her and took her hands in his. "Listen to me, baby. Your father, Tim, and Jay are responsible for their own shit. You've done nothing wrong; you have nothing to make up for. Think of your mother—you're just like her. She used to say that your light shined so bright, it would brighten the darkest days. No matter how much your father and brothers tried, they weren't able to extinguish your light."

"Mom was so dramatic." She smiled at him. "She also said you were a protector that had a fire within you. She was right. You fought to keep your family together when everything was stacked up against you and look at you now: a successful businessman with his own company. You and your brothers have made millions out of what some back home thought was a pipe dream. They wagered you'd fail and come running back, but I knew you wouldn't. I knew you'd be successful."

"What other option do you have when you use your parents' entire life insurance to make a dream come true and you have four younger brothers depending on you?" He shrugged his shoulders. "You work hard to make it work."

"You got them out of the city and away from all the shit that could have torn your family apart." Thoughts of what it could have been like if

54

her father would have moved out of the city after everything happened lingered in her mind and she looked down at their hands. His thumb caressed over her knuckles, soft and reassuring, as if he were trying to let her know he was there for her. "Why do our conversations continue to circle back to my family or the past?"

"That's what brought us together."

"It might have been what brought us together but that kiss had nothing to do with our past."

"Syd—"

The way he whispered her name, so full of desire and something more that she couldn't place, made her want to reach out and touch him. She took her hand from his and brought her finger to his lips, silencing him. "Don't push me away."

"We can't do that again."

"Why?" He rose to stand again and stepped back but before he could answer, she added, "Don't say it's because I'm too young or you're too old."

"Fine. What about the fact that I'm not good for you?" He held his arm out, pointing at something, but she didn't understand what. "Fuck, Syd, you saw my office and you said it yourself earlier: I'm a workaholic. You deserve someone who will put you first. The baggage I come with is extensive. Cyrus might be eighteen now but my duties to him aren't over. Hell, it might never be when it comes to Cain. You deserve someone who is just starting out and has their whole life ahead of them—a life they can make with you. I'm an old man, set in my ways, with work and family to care for."

"When did twenty-eight become old? I must have missed that change. Is it retirement age? Because if so, old man, it would eliminate the workaholic problem," she teased.

"This isn't a joke." He stepped farther back from her. "But if you need more convincing, here's another one. Jay would kill us both if he knew I ever laid a hand on you. And you know what, he'd be right to do so. Your mother asked me to protect you, not force myself on you."

"My mother? When?"

"The same day that picture was taken." He nodded toward the picture frame that was sitting next to her on the bed. "She sent you in to get your sweater so she could talk to me. She knew Jay was starting to follow in Tim's footsteps. It was one of the reasons I wasn't around as much as I had been before. I wasn't into the things he was doing and his new friends were a threat to you. You were her little girl. She was worried about you and wanted me to watch out for you."

"You were sixteen." She shook her head, unable to believe her mother had asked a teenager to look out for her. He was a kid, with enough of his own stuff going on; he didn't need the responsibility of watching out for his friend's baby sister.

"And wise beyond my years. I knew Jay was up to no good and distanced myself from him. We no longer hung out daily, but you saw me a few times a week. I wanted to make sure you weren't letting him influence you. Sydney, I care about you. I always have."

"You know how I feel because I asked you to marry me when I was six. Nothing has changed. I've loved you then and I still love you." She hadn't planned to tell him that she loved him but it came out before she could think it through. Now, her words hung heavy in the air between them, leaving tension in their wake.

"Maybe this is my fault. Maybe I was around too much. Maybe I led you on..." He glanced back at the picture. "I don't know where I went wrong but Jay—"

"Screw Jay and screw your bullshit." Anger rushed through her as she rose off the bed. "I can't stand here and listen to your disgraceful comments. I fell in love with you because of who you are. Not because I wanted someone to take care of me, or because you led me on. I was a young girl when my childhood crush developed, but I'm not that same child you left behind."

"Don't I fucking know it." His gaze traveled over her body, desire burning within his eyes. "It still doesn't change the facts. Your mother wouldn't have wanted this."

"Mom would have wanted me happy but either way, she's dead. Dad and Tim are in prison, and Jay's about to join them behind bars, possibly for life. None of them matter. What matters is, what do you want?" Her heart pounded against her chest, terrified that he would tell her that he wanted nothing to do with her. She saw desire in his eyes but maybe she was misreading the situation. Then another fear sprang to life within her as she waited for him to answer. "Is there someone else? Are you…um…dating someone?"

He shook his head. "No woman would put up with the hours I work and until a few months ago, I was still the legal guardian of a minor. Any woman who looks at me can see I want stability, marriage, and maybe even a family of my own."

"You're starting to sound like a woman," she teased. "Kids? I thought you'd have your fill of that after taking over with your brothers."

"I look at them as my test run. I screwed up with them enough that hopefully now I can get it right with my own kids." He chuckled more to himself, as if remembering the sudden responsibility of being legal guardian to his younger brothers.

Her eyelids drifted shut and she could see him with a baby in his arms. He stood in a nursery, a big smile on his face as he gently rocked his child to sleep. The love in his eyes when he looked down at the child made her heart bloom. She wanted that to be her child in his arms. *Their* child.

"See what I mean when I say I'm too old for you? We're at different stages in our lives. This is your time to be wild and free." Their gazes met and all she could see was sadness shining through the darkness in his eyes.

"Maybe you don't know me as well as I thought." Her chest tightened, making it hard to breathe. If there was one person who knew her inside and out, she believed it was him. Yet now he stood there and the words coming out of his mouth made her doubt this.

"Syd, that's not what I mean. I want what's best for you." He turned toward the walk in closet. "I'll get some clothes and shower."

"Wait, Coal." She crossed the room and placed her hand on his arm. "You didn't ask but I'll tell you anyway. I want to get out of the city, away from the drugs and crime, away from all the people who know my family, who think I'm no better than them. I want a little place of my own with a husband and a couple of kids. But most of all, I want you."

Chapter Six

At a loss as how to handle being in a constant state of desire and need, Coal threw himself into his work. There was no doubt that he wanted Sydney, but that wasn't why he'd gone to Pittsburgh to bring her back with him. He had gone because she was a friend, someone he cared for, and she didn't deserve the fate Jay had left her to. Innocent girl born into the wrong family, when she deserved so much better. He wanted to show her how life could be. He'd help her start over again, anywhere she wanted to go, but in order to do that, he had to keep his hands off her. If he laid a hand on her, he knew he wouldn't let her go.

Cay strolled into Coal's office and took a seat in the chair in front of the door. "Where is she?"

"Upstairs." He leaned back in his leather office chair and looked at the next oldest of the Tanner brothers. "Why? Did you find something out?"

"I got someone working on it. Most likely won't know anything until tonight. You know how they work; they prefer the cover of darkness. How's she doing?"

"Angry, scared, everything you'd expect." He left out that she wanted more from him than he could give her. With only a little more than two years separating them, Coal and Cay were close, but he still wasn't ready to share that detail with him, or anyone for that matter, yet.

"It's expected that a murder charge will be added later today. I speculate first degree murder, but I can't get confirmation on that yet. At the very least, second degree. Have you prepared her for that, possibly?"

He pinched the bridge of his nose and let out a deep sigh. "When I told her Jay was found with the murder weapon, she wasn't surprised. She believes Jay's responsible and it's inevitable that the charges will come down. She's bracing herself for him to join her brother and father."

"Have you considered what having her here could do to Cain?" Cay kept his gaze on Coal, not giving any indication whether or not he thought having her there was a bad thing.

"I told her to stay away from him." It wouldn't solve the problem in the long run but it was the best he could do for now. "Have you spoken with Cal and Cyrus? Any issues I should be aware of?"

"They're fine. What happened wasn't her fault. She's innocent in all of this. Cyrus feels bad for her. She lost as much as we did but she didn't have someone to pull her out of the grief and heartache. She had to stay in the city, surrounded by everyone that already looked down at her because of her family's dealings. Tim's charges only made their disgust for her worse. She didn't have someone like you to see her through like we did."

"My trial run." Coal grinned as the earlier conversation with Sydney ran through his thoughts.

"Huh?"

"Something that came up when talking with Sydney this morning. She was surprised I wanted a family of my own after having to take over for our parents."

"Well, brother, you did damn fine. I was twenty-one and thought I knew it all. Partying every night, a different girl on my arm each week. I was living the life I thought I wanted." He shook his head as if shaking away those memories. "When everything changed I realized it wasn't what I wanted."

"You became an old man right along with me," Coal teased. "Now to find you a wife so you can settle down like you want."

"There's plenty of time for that." Cay let out a deep laugh and shook his head. "I'm not that eager. I'd rather wait for the right woman than rush into a disaster. On the verge of sounding like a woman, I want what Mom and Dad had. They were happy and in love until the day they died. That's what marriage is about. Too many people we know have had shitty childhoods because their parents hated each other."

"They died together." Coal could picture his parents in his mind, smiling and full of life. "They would have wanted that. Neither one of them left behind to grieve."

"I can second that, but I don't think either would have wanted things to happen how they happened, or leave behind three minor children. If it had been up to me, Cal, Cain, and Cyrus would have been separated and sent off to foster homes. I just wasn't responsible enough."

"You came around and did what needed to be done. You worked your ass off when we started Tanner Cycles and we saw to the others. I couldn't have done half this shit without you." Coal was grateful Cay had been a legal adult and therefore able to help him. Otherwise, with three teenagers, he might have gone insane and no doubt would have had a head full of gray hair by now.

"Cay? You up there?" The youngest brother, Cyrus, called from the stairs.

"Yeah." Cay answered as Cyrus came strolling into the office. "What's up?"

"Tank's looking for you." Cyrus leaned against the wall and glanced over at Coal. "Where is she? I wasn't nearly as friendly with her as you were but I should at least welcome her to our humble home. Maybe she'd be more comfortable over at our house. She can have my room."

"With you in it, I suppose." Cay shook his head. "Not a chance, little brother. You're the last thing she needs."

"What's that supposed to mean?" His eyes widened with shock. "I'll have you know I'm being a perfect gentleman. I just thought after Coal broke her heart it was too much of a strain for her to be forced to share his place. Come on, there's not even a guest bedroom for her."

"Broke her heart?" Confusion had Coal's eyebrows knitted together.

"Come on, Coal. You had to know she had a huge crush on you."

"She was thirteen," Cay reminded the youngest of the brothers.

"Doesn't matter." Cyrus shrugged his shoulders. "We had classes together and I remember the doodles on her notebook with Coal's name through the hearts."

"Enough." Coal didn't want to have this conversation any longer. He hadn't realized that her feelings for him had been so obvious to everyone else. Maybe he shouldn't have spent the time he did with her—she'd been just a child—but it was too late to go back now. "She's not going anywhere. She'll stay upstairs with me and I want you all on alert. Tank will be staying at the house until we're sure no one knows she's here and there is no threat to her safety. Cay and I will go speak with Cain shortly and make sure he knows what's happening. He roams the area at night when he can't sleep, so he'll be able to keep an eye out."

"What's the plan if Jay's convicted?" Cyrus questioned.

"I'll help her no matter what she plans. If she wants to stay here, she can. Or she can go anywhere in the world. I'd hate to see her go back to Pittsburgh, but if that's what she wants…" He almost said he'd support her decision but he knew he wouldn't. He'd fight her tooth and nail to keep her from going back and facing those people and the temptation of making a quick buck like her brothers had. He was her protector and that's what he was determined to do, even if that meant he had to protect her from herself. *Or from me.*

The soft patter of her footsteps on the stairs stopped his thoughts from venturing down a road that would leave him wanting more. He wanted her in his arms and in his bed, but there was so much she deserved that he couldn't give her. The baggage that came with him was too heavy to force on her. He had to make sure things stayed strictly platonic between them; anything more would ruin the friendship they'd had for years.

"Coal, I—" The rest of her sentence died on her lips as she caught sight of Cay and Cyrus in his office. "I'm sorry. I shouldn't have…"

"Don't be bashful. Come on in." Cay gave her the same coy smile that seemed to work on all the ladies. "You might not remember us as well as you do Coal. I'm Cayson—everyone calls me Cay. And this is the youngest—"

"Cyrus." She cut him off. "While I know Coal and Cyrus better than the rest of you, I remember everyone. I can let you get back to your meeting."

"There's no reason to go back upstairs. We were just bullshitting. Come here." Unable to stop himself, he held his hand out toward her, beckoning her. Timidly, she came to him and when she did, he took her hand in his. He wasn't sure if he was offering her comfort to lessen her uneasiness or if it was for his benefit. "I was thinking it would be nice for you to catch up with Cyrus. After all you two went to school together for years. How about we order Chinese food and the five of us catch up?"

"I haven't had Chinese food in ages."

"Then it's settled." He glanced back at his brothers. "Now get back to work."

"Yes, sir." Cyrus gave him a mock salute and turned to leave.

"I'll run into town and pick up the food around six. Do you want to do it upstairs or at the house?" Cay rose from his chair but didn't step away from the desk.

"Upstairs." Now that the plans had been made, Coal wanted nothing more than to cancel them. Even though he knew it would be hard to keep his hands off Syd, he wanted to be alone with her. He wanted her undivided attention. But a night with his brothers around would ease the tension and keep things platonic, just as they needed to stay.

"See you then." Cay strolled from the room, leaving them alone.

"Coal?"

He glanced up at her and the sadness in her gaze made him want to pull her down into his lap. "What's wrong?"

"I can't sit around and do nothing. Whatever the outcome is for Jay, worrying won't change it. Worrying over whoever's after me isn't going to stop them and facing them head on will get me killed." Pulling her hand out of his, she took a step back.

"We're working on it. Just give us time," he reassured her.

"In the meantime, I need something to do." She glanced at his desk and then back at him. "It's obvious that you need some help. So let me help. I can do accounting and ordering. I've done it before. Whatever else you need done, I can learn."

"You don't have to do this."

"I know. I want to. Just give me access to a computer and I'll get started. You won't even know I'm here and you can work on whatever you need to do." When he shook his head, she quickly added, "You got behind coming to fetch me. Let me help you."

"I don't want you to feel like you owe me something because you don't." He needed the help, but having her work with him might be more temptation than he could handle. "You're right, I could use the help. The personal assistant I hired quit on me after only a few weeks."

"Sexual attraction which you denied?" She raised an eyebrow at him.

Her eyes narrowed as she waited for him to answer and he noted a twinge of jealousy in the way her pupils became larger. "No. She quickly grew tired of my hours."

"Really?" She didn't seem to buy his explanation.

"I expected my personal assistant to work my hours, not the other way around. I don't have time to work around her schedule. If I need someone here to answer the phones, deal with ordering, or whatever else I need done, then I expect her here. While she's here I expect her to be working, not fiddling with her nails or texting. You might find I'm a tough boss."

"I wouldn't expect anything else from you." She shot him a quick smile. "You've put everything you had into this business. You've breathed the life into it. To have someone who doesn't put forth the effort that is required to get the job done isn't what you need. It will only create more work for you."

He figured he should turn down her offer to help but he couldn't. Spending time with her, even if it had to be while they were both working, would be better than sitting there in his office with his thoughts on what she was doing upstairs. "I could use the help."

"Then it's settled. Where do you want me to start?" She looked down at the stacks of papers littering his desk. "Exactly how long has it been since your assistant quit?"

"Uh…" He glanced at the computer screen to check the date. "Nine weeks ago."

"No wonder there's so much backlog. Haven't you dealt with any of it?"

"Not nearly as much as I should have. But hey, at least it's stacked in categories." He pointed to the stack farthest away. "Orders, accounting, upcoming projects, complete projects, and well, this one is for things that either don't fit any of the other categories or ones I just stuck there because I didn't have time to deal with them." That pile was the tallest and he grabbed the pages, trying to make them as orderly as the others.

"I hate to throw you out of your office but it might be easier if you let me take over the desk and make heads or tails of all of this." She turned back to the dark wood filing cabinet behind him. It was long instead of tall, and ran the length of the wall behind the matching desk. "Should I expect to find the filing cabinets in the same state?"

He shook his head. "That was organized by Cyrus before I hired the assistant. He used to do the filing after school but now that he's graduated, he's working on restoration projects full time and doesn't have time to do office work for me. I didn't want to mess up the system he worked so hard to put together so I've been piling everything up."

"Well that's not working very well for you now, is it? You need room to work and if you're not organized you're going to end up not ordering a part, or missing a deadline. I'm sure you can find something to do while I start on this, and I'll set anything aside that I have questions on."

"Bossy little thing, aren't you?" He turned back to the computer, clicked a few buttons, and then nodded. "This is the accounting software; anything on the desk most likely needs to be added into that. Besides, in this pile all the orders have been taken care of and while you deal with the mess, I'll work on these other orders." He grabbed the pile of papers and the laptop that he had sitting on his desk. "If you need anything, I'll be right here."

"Here?" She raised an eyebrow at him.

"Yeah, I'll take the sofa. The orders shouldn't take too long and I'm waiting for a call. Why, are you trying to get rid of me?"

"Never." Her voice was barely above a whisper.

"Thank you, Syd." He rose from his chair and as he made his way to the sofa, he brushed past her, making sure that his hand caressed along hers. The simple touch was enough to have the desire burning within him again. His body was pulling him one way while his head warned him against the notion that she was his. She was the woman he wanted, the one who would make his life complete.

It had taken hours to make the small dent in the paperwork but now that Sydney had made sense of what needed to be done, things would go quicker. She leaned over the filing cabinet, filing away the stuff she had already dealt with when Coal's arms slid around her waist and he gently pulled her against his body. Feeling his strong arms wrapped around her, she wanted to sink back into his embrace and see where things would go.

"This can wait, baby. Cal will be here with the food shortly. Why don't we go upstairs?"

She leaned back into him, resting her head on his chest. "I can keep working until he gets here."

"No you can't." He squeezed her tighter to him. "I can't take the lure any longer. I need a cold shower and I don't want you down here by yourself. Not until we know no one followed us." He nipped the curve of her shoulder with his teeth. "Don't fight me on this."

"Then don't fight me on what I know we both want." She dropped the papers onto the filing cabinet and spun around in his arms, letting her hand fall onto his toned chest before sliding it down toward his manhood.

"Syd…" His tone held a mixture of desire and warning.

"What?" she questioned innocently.

"You need to think about what you're doing." He pressed her tighter against him, making sure she felt the effect she had on him. "I'm a man with limitations. Don't push me, baby."

She looked him in the eyes and slowly licked her lips. "I want to break those limitations. I know you don't want to believe it but I want you, Coal."

"Sydney, my sweet Syd, you have no idea what hearing you say that does to me."

"I think I do." She reached down between them, sliding her hand over his manhood. She wanted to slip it under the rough material of his jeans and feel the hardened rod in her hands without anything in the way.

"That's only part of it." He tipped his head and nuzzled it between her neck and collarbone. "Baby, you do things to me that I've never experienced before. You make me want to say things I never thought I'd say to a woman. I can't deny that I want you—you feel the evidence in your hand as to what you do to me—but if we venture down that road it will surely lead us straight to Hell. I want this to be about more than just sex."

"I love you, Coal. I always have and always will. I'll gladly buy a one-way ticket to Hell if it means I can spend my life with you."

"Before we punch our tickets, let's spend some time together. The boy you fell in love with is a different man now. I've changed since our days at the park and the nights in your yard looking up at the stars. I had to grow up in order to take care of my brothers. Tonight, we'll spend it with them; it will be relaxing and will give you a chance to see everyone again. Tomorrow…well, let's just start with tonight and go from there."

She wanted to argue, to tell him that he hadn't changed, but, like her, she knew he had. Not all changes were bad. Through their email exchanges, she was aware he'd grown into the man who now stood before her. He'd experienced hardships when it came to raising his brothers and starting

Tanner Cycles, but he'd made it through them and came out stronger in the end. She'd give him this time to accept what was happening between them and in the end, it would make them a stronger couple. Their love would see them through.

"Food!" Cay hollered.

"So much for that cold shower." Coal shook his head and stepped back from her. "We're just finishing up in here."

Coal barely got the words out when Cay, Callaway, and Cyrus walked into the room. Cay and Callaway each had two heavy bags of food in their hands, while Cyrus carried a bottle of soda.

"Oh man, tell me you haven't put her to work on this mess." Callaway looked at his oldest brother. "What are you thinking? You'll have her running out of here."

"I volunteered," she explained, not wanting them to think that Coal had forced her into it. "I've never been able to just sit around doing nothing, so why not help where I can? I have accounting experience so I thought this is where I would be of most use. I know nothing about motorcycles or old cars, which makes it difficult for me to assist you guys downstairs."

"Let's go upstairs and eat before the food gets cold." Coal tipped his head toward her and she led the way. "Earlier I made sure there was plenty of cold beer in the fridge."

"Sydney, I hope you like the soda I grabbed. Coal never keeps much on hand besides beer." Cyrus added as they began to climb the stairs.

"No alcohol for you, Cyrus, and I don't want to catch you in the liquor cabinet again." Cay laughed.

"That was nearly a year ago," Cyrus growled as if he was offended that it was brought up, but he had a smile on his face. "Hell, it was worth it. It helped to loosen Anna's tongue."

"Shut up, Cyrus!" Cay hollered but his voice sounded too far away to be right behind them.

When Sydney reached the top of the stairs she turned back and could see Cay and Coal still in the office. They stood close together, their voices hushed so she couldn't hear them. Fear crept into her muscles. Had Cay learned something? What if they weren't able to take care of the people after her? Maybe the murder charge had been added to Jay's list of charges.

"Come on." Cal touched her arm. "Let's get the food ready."

"What's happening?" She looked up at Callaway but couldn't read his face.

"I don't know, but worrying isn't going to help anything. What's happening with your brother isn't going to change if you worry yourself sick. I'm sure Coal will tell you later. Now come on."

Before Cal could force her away from the stairs, Coal glanced up at her. Sadness lingered in his eyes, before he forced himself to smile. She wanted to run down the stairs and demand that they tell her what was happening. What if it wasn't about her or Jay? Maybe it was work related and none of her business. Even as she thought this, she knew it wasn't what they were talking about. Their voices were too low, Coal's fists tightened with anger, and the sadness in his eyes... Whatever they were discussing, it was about her. Surely, she had a right to know.

"So, Sydney..." Cyrus handed her one of the two glasses of soda he had poured. "Dating anyone?"

"Casanova, she's off limits." Coal appeared at the top of the stairs, his gaze on her.

Off limits because I'm yours or because you don't want anyone else to have me?

70

Chapter Seven

The evening surrounded by his brothers should have been relaxing for Coal but the tension ate away at his stomach, making it hard to concentrate on the conversations around him. His gaze slid over to Sydney every few moments, as if reassuring himself that she was really there. The connection between them was more than friendship; he wanted her but more than that, he wanted her safe.

The group after her hadn't returned their calls to make a trade—the money Jay owed them in exchange for them leaving Sydney alone. It could mean they weren't interested but he tried not to read too much into it. Maybe they were busy with something else. He didn't want to think of the possibility that they might already be in Minnesota. She was safe there.

This place was well protected—a ten-foot tall, electric fence surrounded their entire property, and cameras monitored every inch with the stream fed to his home and office, as well as his brother's house and Cain's cabin. Alerts would be sent to all their cell phones if there was a breach. Some thought it was overkill but when they'd had a customer's rare bike nearly stolen from their lot, they'd made the changes. The bikes and old cars they had around the shop were worth too much not only financially but in sentimental value to their customers to be willing to take a chance on. Now that Sydney was there, he was thankful for the extra security.

"Coal," Sydney called to him as she made her way down the stairs. Fresh from the shower, her long blonde hair fell wild with soft curls around her shoulders. She had changed into a pair of black yoga pants and a tank top that hugged her curves and breasts. "I was hoping you'd tell me instead of having to ask but I can't wait any longer. What did Cay say to you earlier? Did he find out something?"

"Come here." He sat up from where he was stretched out on the sofa and muted the television, losing interest in the news reports. "What did you hear?"

"Nothing." She sank down next to him on the sofa. "I wish I had but I hadn't even realized you weren't behind me until Cay hollered at Cyrus about drinking."

"We weren't trying to hide it from you." He slipped his arm around her shoulders, pulling her back against him. "Cay didn't want to alert Cal and Cyrus; that's why he pulled me aside. He wanted us to have a good evening without the weight of the future hanging above us. We hoped that an evening with friends would keep your mind off everything that's happening."

"Then it is about me? I was hoping you'd say it had something to do with work." Her smile disappeared as she looked up at him, expecting the worst.

"We haven't been able to make contact with those after you but I have people still trying. We'll get to the bottom of it but until then, you're safe here. You saw the security when we drove up. No one can get past the main gate unless we allow them in."

"But that's not all of it." She snuggled against him and wrapped her arm across his front. "Tonight I'd catch you looking at me when you didn't think I was watching you and I'd see sorrow shining in your dark brown eyes. That tells me there's something more."

72

"The district attorney is expected to add first degree murder charges at noon tomorrow unless Jay takes the plea bargain they have on the table." He ran his hand down her arm. "I'm sorry, baby."

"He knew what would happen if he continued along the path he was on, but he refused to give up the quick money for a nine-to-five job. Whenever I would pressure him to give it up, he told me he couldn't. They wouldn't just let him walk away from it all. But he said not to worry because nothing would happen to him. He believed he was invincible."

He sat in silence for a few minutes, letting things sink in before he made the offer he wasn't sure he wanted to make. The only reason he contemplated the offer was for her, not for Jay. Jay didn't deserve it, but he'd do anything in his power to ensure Syd's happiness.

"I could hire him an attorney, one that could get him—"

"No!" She pulled out his arms and scooted to the end edge of the sofa. "I couldn't...you couldn't...no, just no."

"Syd, baby..." He placed his hand on her shoulder, tugging just enough for her to look back at him. "I was thinking of you with that offer. The public defender he has is useless. He couldn't care less if Jay is convicted or not. From what I've gathered, he's pressing Jay to take the deal the district attorney is offering."

"I couldn't live with myself knowing I allowed you to hire someone to get him off."

"If you're worried about the money—"

"That's not it. Actually, I hadn't even considered that yet, but yeah it would be an issue." She dragged her hands through her hair, pushing it out of her face. "I couldn't live with knowing we had something to do with getting him off. I want him to have a fair trial but I know he's guilty so I can't stand by and allow you to help free him. He deserves to be in prison.

This time he killed another drug dealer, but what if the next time he loses his temper, an innocent child or bystander happens to be in the way?"

"Syd, you need to know they must have a strong case because the deal on the table is for a minimum of twenty years before he's eligible for parole, thirty if he does the full sentence. It's a lengthy sentence but it's better than life in prison without parole." He leaned forward, letting their gazes meet. "Are you able to stand by when you might never see him outside of a cage again?"

Tears threatening to fall, she nodded. "How many have to die before my family is stopped? Tim, Dad, and now, Jay. I can't take anymore. I haven't been to see either of them since they were convicted and I don't even want to face Jay. I can't look him in the eyes without hatred consuming me for what he did to me. I'm the one that might have to pay the price for his crimes."

"Okay, baby." He pulled her back against him, rubbing his hand in small circles along her back, comforting her. "We'll let things play out as they might."

"You've bailed him out before." It wasn't so much of a question as a statement she made as she leaned against him. She wasn't cuddled against him as she had been before, but having her in his arms was better than the alternative.

"Not for the past couple of years." He tangled his hand through her hair, enjoying the feeling of the silky strands sliding through his fingers. "I could see the change in him. The charges were escalating and I was distancing myself from him. I didn't need that shit in my life."

"I wish I had that option."

"You do now." He pressed his lips to the top of her head. "No matter what happens over the next few days, whenever this is over, I'll help you. If you want to start over around here or somewhere else, I'll help you. You're not alone. You don't only have me but also my brothers. We'll always be there for you."

"It's been a long few days. We're both tired. Come upstairs with me."

Every fiber of his body wanted to say yes to her but he knew it wasn't that easy. "Syd, you need to think about this. Seriously think."

"I just want you to hold me while I sleep. We could both use a good night's sleep. Please, Coal. I want to feel your body against mine and block out everything else."

Relenting, he nodded. "Let's go upstairs. We'll face everything else in the morning, *together*."

He realized as they rose from the sofa, hand in hand, and headed toward the loft bedroom, he wasn't willing to give her up if they had a chance. She wanted him and he wanted her; the rest was just details. They had the odds stacked against them, but so had he after his parents were killed. Rather than crack under the pressure, the experience had made him work that much harder to make sure they made it through. They could do it together.

Thoughts ran through his head as he wondered how his brothers would take the news that he was in love with Sydney. The disappointment in Cyrus's face when Coal had told him earlier Sydney was off limits crossed his mind. He'd be disappointed he didn't have a chance with her, but other than that, Coal figured the rest of them would take it well. He knew Jay wouldn't be happy with it but since he was looking at a long prison sentence, it didn't really matter what he thought.

He had convinced himself they could overcome one problem but as they walked past the entry way, he caught sight of their reflection in the mirror. This reminded him there was still another problem that might not be overcome as quickly. While she'd said she wanted a husband and kids, he wasn't convinced she was ready for all of that. She was eighteen years old, with her whole life ahead of her—college or just partying with friends—and he had ten years on her. He was too old to spend his nights partying and he didn't want to be the cause of tying her down with a family she didn't want. Hell, even if he didn't want children of his own, he still felt responsible for his brothers, even if they were all legal adults now.

There are so many things I can't give her that someone her own age could. She deserves so much better than me. I come with too much baggage.

A week passed with Coal and Sydney working side by side in his office and falling to sleep cuddled in bed together. They had been unable to work out a deal with the drug dealers Jay owed money to but as of yet, they'd had no issues with them. Cay's research determined that the police were working on closing in on the dealers. If they ended up behind bars, it would eliminate one problem—and thanks to a tip Cay had stumbled upon, it was looking like the police would be getting to them within forty-eight hours.

After turning down the plea bargain, first degree murder charges had been added to Jay's extensive list of indictments. Syd had taken the news better than he thought and had stuck by her original comment, refusing to allow him to hire a good attorney for her brother. He wouldn't have done it for his friendship with Jay but for her he'd do anything in his power to make her happy.

"Hello, Tanner Cycles. How can I help you?"

Her sweet voice drifted toward him, pulling him out of his thoughts, making him look over at her. She sat behind his desk, still working her way thought the piles of paperwork. The once cluttered surface was now clean. She had worked every day, making a dent in the backlog and now only a small stack remained. By the end of the day, there was no doubt she'd have that taken care of as well.

"Yes, sir. Actually, I just received an update. The part Cal was searching for has been found. We've sent someone to retrieve it this morning. Once we have it here, your motorcycle should be complete within two days. I can have Cal give you a call this afternoon if you'd like to speak with him."

He sat his laptop on the sofa next to him and leaned forward, listening carefully to how she handled Hawk Applegate. So far she seemed to be handling the call on her own but she was just learning their business and if he needed to take over the conversation, he wanted to be ready. Hawk was one of their steady customers. He owned a bike shop in South Dakota. Occasionally, he'd pick up bikes on the cheap and had them restore it for his shop; other times he was just looking for something special to showcase. His place was in the center of a biker town, and he kept a window especially for Tanner Cycles, always putting one of their bikes on display. This worked out for both of them and there was little delay in one of the motorcycles selling.

"Yes, sir. I understand, I'll have him call you once it's complete with shipping details. Thank you."

A grin stretched across his face as she wrapped up the call. She was becoming a valuable part of this team. With her help around the office, he was able to focus on some of the tasks that he'd neglected. The best part was, he'd had time to search out two older bikes that they'd restore, as well as work on a couple of custom designs for bikes they'd build. That had always been the highlight of his work. He only dealt with the accountant side of things because he had to. He was too much of a control freak to hand it off to just anyone. He needed to trust them, as he trusted Syd.

"What are you grinning about?" Her gaze was on him as she slid the phone back into the cradle.

"Hawk Applegate is a valued customer. We have an arrangement with him that often brings the shop custom jobs. You handled him well." He realized he'd never let anyone handle Hawk before. Previous assistants knew that when Hawk called, he was to be transferred to Coal's office immediately.

"Maybe I've finally found my calling." She shot him a playful grin and tucked a stand of her hair behind her ear. "Now I thought you were working."

"Forget work." He rose off the sofa to come to stand next to her. Taking her hand in his, he pulled her up against him. "Go get ready. We're going to have a night on the town and a romantic dinner at one of my favorite restaurants in Minneapolis."

"Are you sure it's safe?"

"Don't worry, baby." He wrapped his arms around her waist. "I'll always keep you safe. Now go get ready."

She nodded and he let her slip out of his grip to go upstairs. The moment she was gone, he cursed himself for thinking they could work. That somehow their friendship would find a way to make a relationship work. She was too good for him but that didn't stop him from wanting her. "What the fuck am I doing?"

"I thought you weren't going to doubt us."

He turned to find Syd leaning against the doorframe. "I thought you were getting ready."

"I started upstairs when I heard you curse and I knew you were having doubts. Coal, I want this. I want us. We can make this work."

"It won't be easy." He dragged his hand over his face. Maybe it wouldn't be as hard as it could be, especially with Jay facing the prison sentence that he was, but they'd still have their battles. He wasn't yet completely sure how his brothers would take the news.

She wandered over to him, her body brushing against the front of his as she interlaced their fingers. "The best things in life are worth fighting for."

"So young. So innocent. I wish I still had your faith." He leaned down, their foreheads touching, and their gazes locked on each other. "You make me want to throw caution to the wind and tell everyone to fuck off."

"Then do it," she urged. "But please, Coal, you can't keep pulling me close and then pushing me away. I can't take that. Not again, not from you. If you don't want this, tell me. I'm a big girl. It will hurt but I can handle it. What I can't handle is this push and pull."

"You have no idea how much I want you. But it's not that easy. My brothers...the company...your family—"

"Fuck my family."

A deep, uncontrollable laughter vibrated through him. To hear her drop the F word sent him back years ago. "Do you remember the first time you said fuck?"

"Momma was so livid, she almost skinned me alive. Tim and Jay got in trouble because of it. Little did she know, I'd actually picked it up from you. Tim and Jay were too careful not to say it around the house, they knew Dad would gut them where they stood if he heard them swear. Dad swore like a trucker but he wouldn't allow his boys to pick up his bad habits."

"That's when I knew I was spending too much time around you. Eighteen with my first motorcycle, I thought I was a tough guy with an attitude. Until I realized it wasn't what life was about. Family, that's what's important."

"You were always there for your family, and for me, too. You were always the one constant in my life, the one person I could always rely on." She stepped back and gave his hand a gentle tug. "Come up with me."

"Go on, baby. I'm going to speak with Cay and then I'll be up." He took his hands out of hers and hooked his arm around her waist, tugging her back against his body. "You feel right here, like you were always meant to be." He pressed his lips to hers, quick but enough to make his cock harden instantly.

Images of pushing her back onto the desk and fucking her until she screamed his name flashed before his eyes but that wasn't how he wanted their first time to be. *Shit, when did I decide I was going to fuck her? She's going to be the death of me.*

"Go on, I'll be up in a few minutes." He needed a few minutes away from her if they were going to make it to dinner. He stepped back and pressed the intercom button allowing his brothers to hear him down in the workshop. "Cay, can you come up here for a minute?"

When he let go of the button, she rose up onto her tippy toes and kissed his cheek. "Don't be too long."

"I won't, baby." He'd make the conversation with his brother quick so he could get back to her. Alone and away from the constant reminder of his commitments to his family and the business, they could spend time just being together, without the interruptions or stress. Two people, hopeful lovers, with their lives ahead of them. *Fuck! She's turning me into a romantic.*

# Chapter Eight

It was nearly midnight when Sydney and Coal made it back to his place and she still didn't want the evening to end. They made it to the living room before she spun around to face him. Taking his tie into her hand, she tugged him closer. "Coal…"

"Yeah, baby?" He slid his hands around, running them up her back.

"I want you." She tried to stop the butterflies from circling her stomach but they only intensified as he stared down at her. "I'm tired of waiting. I want more than just you sleeping next to me. I want you to make love to me."

"There's no going back from this." Even as he spoke, he found the dress' zipper between her shoulder blades and teased it down, one notch at a time. "You have to be sure this is what you want, Sydney. Once I've buried my cock between your legs, I'm never going to get enough of you. I'll want you to scream my name every night; hell, multiple times a day. I'll want you in my life, always."

"It's what I've always wanted." She loosened the knot in his tie as the urge to get him naked burned within her. "You're the only man I've ever wanted. I want you by my side every day and cuddled against me every night. I want to have your children. But most of all, I want you. I love you, Coal Tanner."

"My sweet Syd. I've always loved you. First as a little sister, then as a friend, and now for the woman you've become. You've always been remarkable, but now you're amazing. I love you, Sydney." With that, he pulled the zipper the rest of the way down, allowing her dress to slip off her shoulders.

She dropped her arms to her side, letting the thin material slide down her body, to pool around her ankles. Standing before him in only her bra and panties, a surge of excitement rushed through her. This was what she wanted and now that it was happening, she was having a hard time believing it. Her Coal...the only man she wanted. What had once been a young girl's crush had developed into something more. She loved him. He was her protector, her best friend, and now her lover. Maybe one day, he'd be her husband. A six-year-old's wish might finally come true.

Looking up at him, their gazes met, and she traced her fingers along the crisp red dress shirt he'd worn for their dinner out. "Let's go upstairs."

"That might be the best idea of the night." He scooped her into his arms and headed for the stairs. "Tonight, on our way back, when we were standing on the hill overlooking the town of Davenport, I wanted to strip your clothes off you and make love to you under the stars."

"Why didn't you?" She hooked her arm around his neck as he climbed the stairs.

"You deserve better than a quick fuck on the overlook. Tonight, baby, I'm going to show you."

"Then, tomorrow, we'll make love on your rooftop terrace with the stars shining down on us." She tenderly brushed fingertips along the curve of his cheek. "I've always wanted to make love under the stars."

"Then we will, baby." He laid her on the bed and stepped back before she could stop him.

"Come back here."

He shook his head and took another step back before unbuttoning his shirt. "Just be patient and I'll give you what you need." In a blink of an eye, he stripped out of his clothes to stand naked as the day he was born.

Wanting to take in the sight of his amazing body better, she rose up onto her elbows. She ached to run her hand along his chest, to feel every chiseled aspect of his toned body and to explore the dark ink that permanently marked his skin. When he stepped toward her, she reached out and touched the curve of his shoulder. In the dim light, she could make out a sun and moon merged together with his parents' initials in it. "It's beautiful and so fitting. Your mom always said that she and your dad were like the sun and the moon."

Almost like reflex, his hand went to the tattoo, gently brushing against hers. "Their differences somehow balanced each other out. She was hotheaded with a temper and a tongue borrowed from Satan himself. Dad was very relaxed and avoided confrontation at any cost. Their differences made them stronger. They had a happy marriage and I never saw them argue."

"I always hoped that one day I'd have what they had. I want a husband who looks at me the way your dad looked at your mom."

"Oh baby, it's good you've been too busy in the office and haven't caught me looking over at you." He reached behind her, unhooked her bra, and stripped it from her in one clean move. "Now enough about my tattoos and the past. Tonight is about you…us."

"Us…" The word came out as a whisper but she hadn't meant for it to be said aloud at all.

If he'd heard her, he didn't comment. He sat down on the bed next to her, his arms wrapped around her waist, then kissed her, a long, slow deliberate kiss that gave and demanded. He cupped her breasts and teased her nipples, gently swirling his thumb against the hard buds and then pinching them. Pain mingled with pleasure and she arched into his body. He abandoned her mouth and kissed her neck, nibbling down her jawline to her shoulder. Slowly, he teased kisses down her chest until he came to her breast and flicked his tongue over her hardened nipple. The pleasure forced a moan from deep within her as she arched toward him. It felt as if every nerve ending in her body was alight with desire; the simplest touches fanned the burning desire within her. Looking up at her, he sucked the nipple into his mouth, allowing his teeth to run along either side, before he let the hardened bud to slip from his lips.

"I love how your body responds to me." He slid into bed next to her as he teased along the curve of her other hip, coming to the hem of her black panties. "These have got to go."

In one quick wiggle, she rose up just enough to slip off the thin material before tossing them off the bed. "Naked never felt so freeing." His gaze traveled over her body, taking all of her in. Nervous, she wrapped her arms around herself.

"Don't, baby." He took hold of her hands, placing them at her sides. "Don't cover yourself. You're beautiful. Every single inch of you."

As if to prove what he meant, he trailed his hand down her body and between her thighs. The caresses of his fingers had her spreading her legs, and her breath caught in her chest. He explored up her inner thigh, ever so slowly, until he could slip his finger between her folds, quickly finding her center and working deep within her. She moaned as he worked a second finger into her. In and out, quicker with every pump. As her climax approached, he slowed, until he stopped altogether.

Even as she wiggled against him, wanting more, he took his time. Easing his way back up the length of her body, he blazed a trail of kisses across her stomach, stroking his fingertips along the curves of her sides. With every touch, she arched her hips into him, demanding more. Yearning coursed through her; she could wait no longer for him to claim her. Her mind lingered in a sexual haze, needing him now.

"Not yet, baby."

"Please, Coal…" she moaned, arching toward him.

"Soon, baby." He pressed his lips to her neck, dragging his teeth along the smooth skin before leaning back. "Answer me honestly. Are you a virgin?"

She shook her head, letting him know that she wasn't, while she tried to keep the memories of the time she'd lost her virginity out of her thoughts. It had been one time, with someone she wanted to care for because he was a good guy and loved her, but she couldn't. Every aspect of him she'd compared to Coal. In the end it hadn't been enough for him to be second fiddle to the memory of a man she'd never had but always loved.

"You don't have to be gentle with me." She reached down and ran her fingers through his hair. "I want you, rough, full of heat, until we're both out of breath."

"Well, Syd, why don't you set the pace?" He rolled off her and onto his back next to her.

"Giving a woman control…I didn't expect that."

"Don't get too used to it. I like to be the one in charge but tonight is all about you. Are you up for the challenge?" Grinning at her, he put his arms behind his head and waited.

Not wasting a moment, she straddled his hips and wrapped her hand around his shaft. Gliding caresses up and down the hard length, she teased his erection harder. He groaned and reached up to caress her breasts. Heat coiled between her thighs and her sex clenched.

"I've been waiting so long for this moment." She loved the feel of him in her hand and knowing she caused his cock to be rock hard. He desired her as much as she wanted him.

"Then let's not waste another second." Even with his suggestion, he did nothing to urge her to move faster.

Desperate, she shifted her position. Angling the head of his cock just below her opening, she sank down onto it, slowly allowing his hardness to fill her inch by inch, until his low moan echoed hers. Moving his arms from behind his head, he reached out and pinched her nipple, the pain mingling with pleasure. She rocked upward and then down again, finding her rhythm. Impatience coiled through her as she tried to find the right motion. As if realizing her frustration, he grasped her hips, increasing his pace and driving into her with force.

With every thrust, he sped his pace, hands on her hips, pulling her down onto him harder and faster. Stroke after stroke, the tempo between them intensified until his hips where slamming off hers. The thrusts became deeper, more urgent, falling into a perfect rhythm. Their bodies rocked back and forth and her back arched, pushing her breasts out toward him as her orgasm neared. The tension strained through her muscles, tightening around his cock.

"Fuck, baby." He dug his fingers into her hips. "Tighten around my cock."

As she pushed down onto him, he arched up to meet her. Ever faster and deeper, they met each other's thrusts. They climbed the mountain, both seeking the apex. "Coal!" Screaming his name, she slammed down onto his body as her orgasm found her. She dragged her nails along his chest, leaving angry red scratches.

His grasp on her hips tightened, keeping his cock buried deep within her as his own orgasm hit him. "Fuck, baby."

She collapsed on top of him, her hands on either side of him, holding him tight to her. This had been what she had wanted and hoped for; but now that she had him, she was terrified he would end up breaking her heart.

If he got up in the morning and regretted their night together, she wasn't sure how she could face him again.

"Syd." He brushed her hair away from her face.

"I'm sorry, I'll get off you."

"No, baby." He wrapped his arms around her, holding her in place. "You can stay there all night if you wish."

"Then I'll stay." She wrapped her lips over his nipple, gently biting it.

"Fuck, baby." His cock twitched inside her, sending a jolt of desire rushing back through her, forcing her inner core muscles to tighten around him again. "Baby, if you do that again I won't be responsible for my actions."

"What will you do?"

"I'll roll you over and fuck you until you're so fucking sore you can't walk straight tomorrow, let alone sit." He swatted her ass, making her jerk in surprise.

"Oh, Coal!" She slipped off him to cuddle beside him. "If I could wake up every morning next to you and have amazing sex like this every night, I think my life would be complete. But if I wake up in the morning and you regret everything that's happened, I will always have tonight to remember."

"Morning will be here before we know it and I can promise you I won't regret this. If making love to you when the sun comes up will prove that to you, I'll do it without a single complaint." He squeezed her tight against his side. "I love you, Syd, and nothing is going to change my mind. You're mine, today, tomorrow, and forever."

Joy and excitement exploded through her chest. *I'm his!* Her excitement diminished when a soft buzz echoed through the loft.

"Fuck." He slipped his arm from around her and shot out of bed, quickly making his way to the smaller model of the security unit on the dresser. He could still see all the cameras and communicate with the gate's speaker box, but it wasn't as nice as the larger model downstairs.

"What's happening?"

He wanted to tell her it was nothing but the Davenport police cruiser outside his gate made him believe otherwise. Rather than lie to her, he shook his head and pressed the intercom button. "Can I help you?"

"Mr. Coal Tanner? I'm Sergeant Scholl and I need to ask you a couple questions."

"Whatever this is about, arrangements can be made through my attorney, Mr. Kevin Ashburn."

"I'd prefer to get it over with now, but if you want to do this the hard way, I can have a warrant here within an hour's time. I just need to clear up some questions concerning Jayden Manor and determine if you know his whereabouts."

"Sergeant, I know where he is. He's in jail in Pennsylvania, waiting for his trial." When Syd stepped up next to him, he let go of the intercom button and he slipped his arm around her, pulling her close to him. "Why are the Davenport Police interested in Jay?"

"It's our belief if he isn't already here then he's on his way to the area in search of his sister. Now are you going to let me in or should I request a warrant?"

"Fuck!" He held her tighter, not wanting to let her go. Due to his charges, Jay had been denied bail, so if he was out and headed this way, it could make for a nasty situation, one he didn't want her in the middle of.

"Don't make trouble for yourself. You haven't done anything wrong. Let him in," Sydney, who had been quiet up until now, urged him.

Without a word, he pressed the button, allowing the gate to swing open and the sergeant to drive in. "Baby, I want you to stay here. I'll meet him downstairs."

"Why? Why would Jay run? With the pending charges and his criminal record, he has to realize they'd use whatever force necessary to take him down."

"I don't know, baby, but I'm going to find out what they know. Meanwhile, I want you to get dressed. If we need to we'll go to the main house. It will be safer with everyone around." He pulled open the drawer and grabbed a pair of jeans before quickly tugging them on.

"You think he'll come after me? Why? It doesn't make sense. We're family." Shivering, she shook her head.

"You told me yourself that he admitted to killing someone. You could be called as a witness and your testimony would no doubt help put him behind bars for a very long time." Opening another drawer, he pulled out two t-shirts, dropped one onto the dresser, and quickly slipped the other one over her head. It was big on her, but it was something to help keep the chill of the air at bay and to stop her from shivering. "Listen to me—it's going to be okay. You're safe here." He'd make sure of it. His brothers and Tank were around for extra protection but he'd make sure to bring in additional security in the morning, not to protect the property but to protect his girl.

"I just want this over." She leaned forward, pressing her forehead against his chest.

"Soon, baby, soon." He kissed the top of her head before he led her back over to the bed and tucked her under the covers. "Just rest. I'll be right back."

He hated to leave her but he wanted to handle Sergeant Scholl himself first to pump whatever information he could get out of him. If the sergeant wanted to question her, he'd have to wait. As he jogged down the stairs, his cell phone, which he'd tossed into his pocket on the way out the door, vibrated with a message from Cay. *Tank's checking the perimeter. What do you want us to do?*

He stopped for a moment in his office, surrounded by memories of the last several days working side by side with Sydney, and shot Cay a quick message back. *Be ready if Jay comes for her.* Jay and her family had done enough to her; he'd be damned if he'd let it continue. She deserved so much better than what they'd put her through. How many times when they were kids had he stepped in to keep her safe because of something her father, Tim, or Jay had gotten into? Too many times; eventually he'd lost track.

The knock on the door to the shop reminded him that Sergeant Scholl was waiting and forced him to finish his descent to the shop. While climbing down the rest of the stairs, he wondered where Jay was. Had he already made it to Minnesota? How long did they have before he made an attempt to get at Syd? Without any answers to the questions floating within his mind, he pulled open the door and stepped out.

"I knew you were a sensible man and would see things my way." The sergeant leaned against the hood of his car. "We're going to do this here or are you going to invite me in?"

"Ask your questions." Coal wandered away from the door, nearing the sergeant who appeared to be tired and overworked.

"On the night of his arrest, Jayden placed his only call to you. Was he hoping you'd bail him out? Hire him a lawyer?" Sergeant Scholl took a small notebook out of his shirt pocket and unclipped the pen, ready to write down anything useful.

"No."

"It's my understanding that you and Mr. Manor go way back. You've even bailed him out before, paid for his lawyers. Why wouldn't you do it again?"

"Because I washed my hands of it." He shoved his hands into the pockets of his jeans. "Jay and I grew up together and I've helped him in the past but he's unwilling to make changes in his life. He wants to stay in the criminal world and I want nothing to do with that. I told him that."

"If he knew all of that then what was the purpose of his call?"

"His sister. But you already know that, don't you?" Coal didn't give the sergeant a chance to answer. "Sydney Manor was in danger because of Jay's criminal dealings. He knew that and asked me to get her out of the city so that she was safe."

"What is her involvement in his dealings?"

"None," Coal growled before he could stop himself. "Sydney's innocent. Born into the wrong family but their crimes are not her burden to carry."

"Let's stop this charade." Scholl shoved his notebook back into his pocket. "We haven't had dealings together because I'm new to this town, but I know of you. The whole department knows you. You know how it is in a small town like this. I was the only one on when the call came through. Chief Kingsworth and Officer Cunningham are on their way."

"Seems like overkill to bring out the chief when all you wanted was a few answers to your questions." Coal raised an eyebrow at the sergeant. "Unless you're planning...oh fuck no! You're not using Syd as bait to catch her lunatic brother."

"She's already in the line of fire. His picture is all over the news and a clerk from a minimart in Minneapolis called it in. She was leaving work when he hijacked her car. Jayden's in the area and he's coming for Ms.

Manor." The sergeant pulled his phone from his pocket and clicked a button, before holding it out toward Coal. "Need further proof?"

There on the screen was a still from a security camera showing Jay behind the wheel of the stolen car. In the background hung a sign for interstate ninety-four. There was no doubt in Coal's mind that Jay was less than an hour away. "When was this taken?"

"More than two hours ago."

"Fuck!" Two hours ago meant he could already be in Davenport. He was most likely close and he was coming for Syd. "He's not getting her!"

"Chief Kingsworth has been in touch with the Pittsburgh police and from what they've gathered from his brother and a cellmate, they believe Jayden will scope out your place tonight and then find some place to lie low until tomorrow. He'll come after her tomorrow."

"So what now? We just wait?" He wasn't sure just sitting around doing nothing would be the best way to keep Sydney safe. He wanted to throw her in his truck and make tracks out of town as fast as he could. There had to be somewhere safe he could take her. Somewhere Jay wouldn't find her. Once he was safely behind bars again, she'd be free to live her life.

"Unless we can find him first, what choice do we have? He makes his move and we take him down. Cunningham is a good officer but he was chosen for this because he won't stand out. It will appear you've hired another worker. He knows his way around motorcycles, spent years working in a shop a few towns over, and even owns a couple of bikes himself. He'll fit the part that needs to be played and he can be close enough to watch the girl."

"I'm not trusting her safety to just your man." He grabbed his cell phone from his pocket and pulled up Maverick's contact information. "I'm going to call my cousin and get him over here. After twenty years in the

Marines, Maverick recently took his retirement. With him, Tank, and my brothers here, I know we can keep her safe."

"Do that if it gives you more confidence but we'll be the ones taking Jay in. All of the Davenport Police Department officers are being alerted to the situation and others, including the Feds, are on their way. You need to remain here and make it look as normal as possible. When Jayden arrives, he needs to feel at ease to make his move."

Chapter Nine

Hours of sitting around talking about her brother coming after her left Sydney cold inside. The very idea that Jay wanted her dead was unbelievable. She couldn't wrap her mind around that but as much as she wanted to protest what they were saying, she couldn't help but wonder if it wasn't true. She could be called to the stand to testify about him coming home that night covered in blood and how she'd witnessed him burning his clothes in the backyard. Her testimony could help put her brother behind bars for life, but even knowing that, she couldn't take responsibility for his conviction. He was the one who'd committed murder, yet, somehow, he was blaming her. That wouldn't make sense to any sane person but her brothers had never taken responsibility for anything they'd done wrong.

"Syd?" Coal wrapped his arm around her shoulders, gently bringing her closer to him.

"Huh?" She blinked and glanced around the room at the men gathered there. All of the Tanner brothers except Cain were present, as well as Coal's cousin, Maverick, Tank, and Officer Cunningham—all of these people willing to protect her. "I don't deserve this."

"Baby." Coal gently rubbed her shoulders, doing his best to soothe her.

"No, I'm right." She swallowed past the lump in her throat. "My family...they're monsters. Jay's killed before. What if this time one of you gets in his line of fire? I can't let you go through with this. Officer Cunningham, there has to be another way, one that doesn't put everyone at risk."

"No fucking way, Sydney!" Coal shot off the sofa, took her hand, and dragged her out of the living area, away from the other men. Without saying a word, he pushed her into the large guest bathroom off the side of the room. With the living area open, the bathroom was the only place where they could have privacy. Even if they went up to the loft bedroom, the others could have overheard them. He shut the door behind them and stepped in front of her, forcing her back against the wall.

"Coal—" She wanted to reason with him, to explain why she should do this on her own, but he wasn't having that.

"Don't, Syd. Just fucking don't!" he growled.

"I don't want to see you get hurt." Even though she wasn't sure that touching him was the best thing, she reached out and placed her hand on his chest. He was angry and while she trusted him completely, she couldn't stop the images of her father's anger lashing out at her mother years ago. Memories of the bruises covering her mother's arms from where her father had grabbed her flashed danced before her eyes. "Please, Coal."

"Please what? Please let you become a target? Please don't be angry that you're willing to risk yourself?" He looked down at her and instantly, the anger in his eyes started to subside. "Fuck, baby, don't look at me like that."

He backed away from her and leaned against the bathroom counter. She stayed pressed against the wall for a moment longer before she took a deep breath. Coal wasn't the same man her father was and she knew he'd never hurt her. The whole situation overwhelmed her and his anger had made the past seep through into their present, but she was about to put an end to that.

"I'm sorry." Wanting the tension to cease and to be in his arms again, she crossed the space to stand in front of him. Even when she put her hands on his chest, his rested on the counter, as if trying to prove to her he wasn't going to hurt her. "I know you'd never hurt me. I don't know why the thoughts even crossed my mind."

"Because your father was an abusive asshole." When her mouth fell open slightly, he nodded. "I saw the bruises on your mother but I remember the rage he took out on Tim and Jay."

"Why was I never at the receiving end? What made me special?"

"Your mother protected you. She'd vowed to leave him and take you and your brothers if he ever raised a hand to you. She wanted to protect all three of you but he told her that she didn't know how to raise a true man, and unless she wanted to lose the kids, she'd let him handle the boys. She was afraid that if she left him, she'd lose you. So she stayed and protected you the best she could."

"I guess us Manor women want to protect those we love." She tried to give him a smile but it was too forced to carry off. If her mother had left her father, maybe she'd still be alive. One thing she knew was that her mother wouldn't have been on the way to fetch her father from the police station, that day when she was killed.

"Well, get that thought out of your head because there's not a chance in hell I'm letting you willingly offer yourself up to Jay. I'll tie you to my bed if I have to, in order to keep you safe."

"Just to keep me safe?" She gave him a quick grin and pressed her body against his. "Something tells me you might get some pleasure out of that."

"You always bring me pleasure."

"What the hell is going on in there?" Cal hollered from the living area. "It's late and if you're not planning on continuing this conversation, all of us would like to get some sleep."

"We'll be out in a minute," Coal hollered to his brother but kept his gaze on her. "Listen to me, baby. I'm not going to allow him to get to you. I'm going to keep you safe and when I hear you saying fucking shit like you told Cunningham, it pisses me off."

"I don't want anything to happen to you." The soft chatter from the other room drifted through the door to her. "I couldn't live with myself if something happened to your brothers because of me."

"Nothing is going to happen. Cunningham is the inside man but there are more watching the area. They're going to take him down before he gets close to us. You have to trust me." He slipped his arm around her waist. "Just like you don't want anyone to get hurt, I don't want anything to happen to you. I love you, Syd, and it would kill me if something happened to you."

She leaned against him and rested her head against his chest. "I can't believe he would do this. Now more charges will be added: escape, grand theft auto, and who knows what else. He'll never get out."

"I know, baby." He held her for a long moment before kissing the top of her head. "We need to get back out there but I don't want to hear any more about you being bait. Understand?"

She nodded and stepped back. "Let's get rid of everyone; for a few hours, I want to forget all about this. I just want to go back to bed with you."

"Go on up. I'll get rid of them and be there in a minute." Keeping his arm around her, they made their way to the bathroom door.

When they stepped through the door, they were met with hoots and hollers from Cal. "Nice of you to join us."

"Go on, baby." He urged her toward the steps and she dashed up.

While things had slowly been progressing between her and Coal, they had yet to bring their relationship to the attention of his brothers. After tonight, she had no doubt they had at least had an inkling that something was happening between them. Her stomach twisted in knots as she wondered how they might take the news. Would they be supportive or would they find fault with their age difference? She and Cyrus were only a few months apart in age. Would he be the one who had the hardest time dealing with her relationship with his brother?

Coal sat in the living room with his brothers. Maverick, Tank and Officer Cunningham had already made their way to main house, giving the brothers a private moment. While he hadn't been hiding what was happening between him and Sydney, he hadn't actually told them about it, either. He just wanted to enjoy his time with her and see where things would go on their own without his brothers' input. While their support was important to him, he wasn't sure how they'd take it. She and Cyrus were the same age and he had already shown interest in getting to know her better. Had he considered taking her out?

"So, you and Sydney?" Cal was the one to break the uneasiness. "Way to go, bro."

"Isn't she a little young for you?" Cyrus asked without even looking at Coal.

Fuck yeah, she is. But he kept his mouth shut, refusing to give Cyrus something to use against him. "What's happening between Syd and me wasn't expected."

"Didn't expect this? Are you serious?" Cyrus snapped, launching off the sofa. "Did you think you could keep your hands off a beautiful woman living in your loft? I told you she had a crush on you years ago and you broke her heart. What kind of bastard sets her up to get hurt again?"

"Cyrus, you need to calm down." Coal eyed his youngest brother. "I know this is unexpected and you're upset but I'd never hurt Syd. She's always been special to me and now that has changed into more. She was thirteen-years-old when you claim I broke her heart. There was absolutely nothing between us back then. Fuck, I was twenty-fucking-three. She was a baby; so were you."

"That doesn't change the fact she was doodling your name all over her notebooks."

"Fine, but we're different people now. We're both adults." Coal looked at Cay and Cal and for a brief moment expected them to join Cyrus' side.

"He's right, Cyrus." Cay put his empty beer bottle aside. "She was a child and you know as well as I do there was nothing besides friendship between them before she arrived here. Now I know you had the idea of getting close to her when she arrived but that's not happening in the way you were hoping."

Coal was more thankful than ever that he hadn't told his brothers about the marriage proposal from six-year-old Sydney. That would have only added more fuel to the fire burning within Cyrus now. He understood where his brother was coming from. Cyrus saw Sydney's arrival as a chance to reconnect with her and see if things had changed enough for him to steal her heart.

"Guys…" Syd stood at the stairs, looking down at them from the loft. "I brought a lot of shit to your doorstep but the last thing I've ever wanted was to come between you. Cyrus, we were friends before, and I'm sorry. If you're angry—fine…but be angry at me, not Coal."

"Syd—"

100

"No, Coal." She glanced back at Cyrus. "You have to understand Coal was against anything happening between us. He wanted to stay in his big brother role, my protector, but I wanted more. You're right, Cyrus. I fell in love with him years ago. Did I ever think I'd be here now with him? Hell, no. But he was the man I've measured every guy up to since I started dating. It wasn't fair to them and maybe that's why it never worked out, but I was unwilling to settle. You have to know that Coal would have never let this happen between us if he knew there was a chance you'd react like this. He'd put you guys first before himself. You guys are the reason I have any idea what family is really about and I don't want to come between you. I'll leave before I allow that to happen."

"That's not going to happen, Sydney," Cal spoke before even Coal could. "Cyrus was shocked by the news and his outburst was unfortunate, especially since you overheard it. You're welcome here and every single one of us will do what we can help you."

"Fuck this. I'm out of here." Cyrus stormed out before anyone could stop him.

"I'll go talk to him." Cal followed after him but before he could leave, he turned back toward Sydney. "Now don't go getting any ideas about leaving us. Cyrus will come around. As long as you and Coal are happy, you have my full support. He deserves a good woman."

"Thanks." She bit her bottom lip as if she wanted to say something else but Cal disappeared down the stairs, leaving them alone.

Silence hung thick in the air and with two of his brothers gone, Coal was just waiting for Cay to say his piece on it. He wanted it all over so he could get back to Sydney before she had time to start overthinking about Cyrus's reaction and blame herself. The youngest of the family had always been the one to let his emotions run his mouth before he had time to consider the consequences.

"Sydney." Cay waited until she turned to glance at him. "Could you give Coal and me a minute?"

"Ahh…sure. I'll just, umm…go get a shower." Her unease showed in the tight muscles and her frantic glances toward Coal, but she quickly disappeared into the loft's bathroom.

With her out of hearing range, he turned to Cay. "If you're about to bitch that she's too young, or any of that shit Cyrus just said, I really don't need to hear it. It's been a long day and we're all tired."

"She *is* young." Cay nodded but did get off the sofa like he was going to leave soon. "But that's not why I wanted to talk to you."

"Then what?" Coal snapped, unable to take his frustration any longer.

"Cyrus had a thing for her, so much that he wanted to ask her out before we left Pittsburgh. He went to do it when he saw your name doodled all over her notebooks, so he knew she wasn't interested. When he heard she was coming, he thought maybe the past had changed and he could make his move."

"How do you know this?" Coal felt like an idiot for not recognizing his brother's attraction to Sydney years ago but now that Cay pointed it out, it made sense. The pieces of the puzzle were falling in place. "She was the girl he was going to ask to his seventh grade dance?" That had been the first actual dance for them and Cyrus had been upset the girl he wanted to take was unavailable, though he'd never told Coal the full details.

"Yeah, I took him to shoot some hops at the gym and he told me about it." Cay went to take a swig from his beer before realizing it was empty. "It's logical that he's upset about how things worked out. He thought maybe this would be his chance. Now he finds out he's out of the game before he even started."

"I'll talk to him in the morning." He wasn't sure what he'd say to his brother to smooth things over but there had to be something. His family was important to him, but so was Syd. They needed to find a balance that worked for everyone.

"First, you need to think about what you're doing. She's a young girl, one who's been through hell and back. I don't want to see you upsetting the balance here just for a quick fuck but most of all, I don't want to see her hurt because you're thinking with your dick."

"Fuck you, Cay." Coal's fingers dug into the arm of the sofa, while his gaze remained on his brother. "She's not a quick fuck."

"I'm just saying she's always cared for you."

"Yeah, I know and I've always cared for her. Not in the same way as I do now but she's always meant a lot to me. You might not believe this but I love her." He wasn't going to get sappy with his brother. While he had to work every day with his brothers and their opinions mattered to him, the one who had to know his feelings for her was Sydney and she was upstairs. "I hope you can respect that."

"Like Cal said, as long as you're both happy." Cay leaned forward, putting his elbows onto his knees. "But have you considered how Cain is going to take this?"

Cain was a wildcard when it came to all of this and while Coal was concerned about it, he also believed it would work out. Cain might have a hard time dealing with it but he wasn't around the family as much as Coal wished him to be. He had become a recluse, refusing to leave his cabin, except at night while everyone was sleeping. He'd have to make it a point to talk to him about this in the coming days but he wasn't about to leave Sydney with Jay out there stalking the grounds. Cain would have to wait until this situation blew over.

"After everything that her brother has done to our family, you know he's going to have a hard time with her presence here," Cay added when Coal remained silent.

103

"I'll deal with him."

"Then there's only one more thing to say." Cay stared at Coal for a moment, his face serious and hard to read. "If you hurt that girl, there's going to be hell to pay. I've never been as close to her as you or Cyrus but she's still family, maybe more now than ever. So know this, I'll knock the shit out of you before you can hurt her."

"You won't have to worry about that." Coal gave his brother a grin. "On the verge of sounding like a gushing female, I'll tell you I think I've been waiting my whole life for her; I just never realized it before. She's everything I've looked for in the woman I want as my wife. She's what I want each of you to find. I want each of you to have the same happiness that I have with her in my life."

"Well, I'll get out of here and you can let her know Cyrus will come around." Cay rose off the sofa and took a step before turning back to Coal. "I should have realized this would happen. There was a change in you once you arrived back with her. She's good for you. Don't do anything to screw it up." Without saying anything further, Cay headed for the stairs, leaving Coal to his thoughts and his woman.

That was what he worried about. Relationships never seemed to work out very well for him. He was too much of a workaholic and women didn't like being deprived of his attention—though the women of his past were nothing like the woman who'd claimed his heart. Sydney knew him on another level, one the other women never got to see. He'd find a way to balance work and romance.

Chapter Ten

Two days had passed and there hadn't been a single sighting of Jay, which made Sydney wonder if he suspected the cops were watching the place. Was he even in the area? Maybe he realized how hard it would be to get to her inside of Coal's compound, so he'd moved on. Maybe he'd left the country in hopes of staying out of prison. All of the possibilities were making her uneasy. She couldn't stand not knowing and the fear growing within only made things worse. The longer Jay stayed on the run, the more likely things would end badly when the police found him.

"This isn't working." Coal tossed a stack of papers onto the corner of the desk and crossed his arms over his chest.

"What?" She blinked up at him, suddenly concerned that she was screwing things up for him. Tanner Cycles was everything to him and her scattered brain was making work harder for him. She needed to step back. "I'm sorry...I didn't mean..."

"What's wrong, baby?" He came around to lean against the desk and took her hand in his.

"I'm distracted...I'm messing up...costing the business..."

"Stop." He pulled her up out of the chair so she was standing before him and wrapped his arms around her waist. "You're fine and that's not what I'm talking about. Sitting around here waiting is killing us. We have to get out of here."

"What if Jay's waiting?"

"Let me worry about that. You know me—your safety is non-negotiable." He ran his hand up her back. "I'll make arrangements while you run upstairs and pack a few things."

"Where are we going? What about work?"

"It's Friday; surely the boss is allowed to knock off a few hours early and spend the weekend away with his lady." He pressed his lips to hers in a quick kiss. "A friend has a condo in downtown Minneapolis. I stay there from time to time when I have business dealings in the city that run late or will take a couple of days. He rarely uses it anymore, so it won't be a problem. There's security in the building."

"Chief Kingsworth and Officer Cunningham aren't going to like this." The moment she said these words, she wished she had kept her mouth shut. The idea of getting away even for a few hours was tempting and the last thing she wanted to do was talk him out of it.

"Don't worry about that. I'll take care of things. Now go get ready; I want to get out of here and have you all to myself."

Without needing any further encouragement, she headed upstairs. Knowing him as she did, she realized he'd have no trouble convincing Chief Kingsworth, and everyone else, that they needed this. They were going to get out of here and live even if it was just for a few hours.

Up in the loft, she stopped by the window and looked out. With the trees surrounding the property and the land that Coal owned, it was hard to see much—but out there, hidden under the cover of the trees, her brother might be lurking, plotting her death. She didn't want to believe it, but she couldn't stop the fear from rising within her. Her family had done some horrible things in the past and while it was Tim who'd dealt them a blow that she had never recovered from, Jay was no different. He was capable of murder and if it would save his own ass, she believed he'd kill her.

"My family is so screwed up." She wasn't sure how long she stood by the window looking out, but she'd had enough of where her thoughts were leading her. Stepping away from the window, she went to gather a few things to take with her. Tonight would be all about the future—not the past and not her family.

Footsteps fell on the stairs to the loft, making her hurry. If Coal had made arrangements that quick, he had to be eager to get away for a bit and she wanted to be ready. They needed some time away from this whole situation and to just spend by themselves. Since the news of Jay's escape, it seemed as if she hadn't been alone with Coal, except when they were either working or exhausted and fell into bed together.

"Sydney?"

The voice had her pausing with her hand on the zipper of the duffle bag. *Cyrus?* After his outburst when he'd learned of her relationship with Coal, she hadn't spoken to him. She saw him around the shop but he was always busy with whatever project he was working on. She hadn't determined if he was ignoring them or was honestly busy, but she hadn't wanted to ask Coal and cause him to worry about the situation. Coming between him and his brothers was something she didn't want but she wasn't sure how to fix things, either.

"Sydney, are you up there? Coal?"

She couldn't hide in the loft forever and she had wanted to talk to him, so this was her chance; she only hoped it would go better than the last time. Leaving the duffle bag where it lay, she crossed over to the railing to look down. "I'm here. If you're looking for Coal, he's not here, but he should be back in his office in a few minutes."

"I'll find him in a few minutes but first could I speak with you?"

Shit. Butterflies circled within her stomach as she descended the stairs. If she was going to stay with Coal, then she'd have to face Cyrus and hopefully get him to see that she cared for his bother. No, 'care' wasn't a strong enough word: she loved him.

As she stepped off the last step, she realized she didn't want to have this fight here. This was the place she shared with Coal and while it had already been tarnished with Cyrus' outburst, she didn't want to have any more negative memories hovering over them. While his brothers had hung out with them there, this had become their own place to retreat. Everywhere she looked she saw positive memories of her time with Coal and the love that they had discovered. "If it's about business, maybe we should go back to the office. I might need to look up whatever you need."

"It's not business." He shook his head and took a step toward her before stopping. "I came to apologize. The things I said were out of line."

"If they are how you feel, then they weren't. You have the right to express your feelings." Even though she wanted to look away, she forced herself to keep her gaze on him. She wasn't about to back down, she had done it too many times in her life. If she wanted him to respect what she had with his brother, she needed to stand her ground. "Cyrus, I always considered you a friend and having you troubled about what's happening is upsetting not just for me but for your brother."

"I know." He wandered over to the sofa and sat down. "Coal stepped up when our parents were killed. He kept us together and raised us. We're lucky to have a brother like him and I'll admit I was an asshole when I found out about you guys. It was a shock."

"To all of us." She stepped away from the stairs, moving closer but not going to the sofa.

"Not to you. You always loved him." He leaned back and looked at her. "You were devastated when he moved us out of the city so he could buy this place and start Tanner Cycles."

"I lost…" She let her words trail off because what she'd lost was mild compared to his loss. She'd lost her mother, but he'd lost both of his parents and nearly lost Cain. She forced herself to finish her thoughts so she didn't have to think about the one Tanner brother she hadn't seen since she arrived. "It was just another blow."

"It was hard on all of us. I gave Coal more trouble than I should have but I realized why he was doing it." He let out a deep breath and shook his head. "It hurt him to leave you behind but he did what was best for the family. Cain…well you know what he went through. The doctors thought a change would help but he's never been the same."

"I'm not sure why you're telling me this." She placed her hand on the cool cement countertop, letting it ground her and keep her from traveling back to the terrible memories he was hinting at.

"We were thirteen, about to have our first school dance, and the only girl I wanted to take was you." He paused for a heartbeat and let that news sink in before leaning forward, his gaze still on her. "When I heard you were coming, I instantly felt like I was thirteen again. I knew your heart already belonged to Coal, but I had hoped something might have changed. While I was waiting to make my move, Coal was making his."

"That's not how it happened. If anyone made the first move, it was me."

"It doesn't matter." He slammed his hand against his thighs, as if the subject was closed.

"It does to me." She stepped away from the counter and went to sit next to him on the sofa. "I've always considered you a friend and I hope we can move past my relationship with your brother to continue that friendship. All of us have been through enough shit. I don't want this to be another obstacle we have to overcome."

"Me either, which is why I came up here tonight. I wanted to apologize." He reached out and laid his hand over hers. "I want you and Coal to be happy; you both deserve it. I don't want to be a chink in things between you two. You already have one with Cain."

"Thanks, Cyrus." Her lips curled into a smile, thinking back to their school days together. They had been fairly close; maybe he'd thought they were closer than she had, but it didn't matter now. He had been a friend, one she had always been able to count on. "I've missed you. I'm sure you have plenty of girls lining up for your attention. In school you always had a line of girls wanting to hang out with you." Too many of them had wanted her to play matchmaker and hook them up with him. She hadn't, not because she'd wanted him to herself as the other girls thought, but because none of them deserved him.

"Yeah, for what they think I can give them." He pulled his hand away and leaned back against the sofa, his eyelids falling shut as he did. "Once Tanner Cycles took off, making the national news, the girls expected the world on a gold platter. It's not my style. I'm not like Coal. I don't fit in at fancy restaurants, and I can't stand when the cameras are around. I'm a jeans and t-shirt guy. I don't want to wear a monkey suit. Grease stains are part of my life because I love my work. I don't want to have to change for a woman."

"You shouldn't have to," she reassured him. "You'll find the perfect girl for you. Don't rush it; it will happen."

"You need to be thinking about what you're going to do, instead of focusing on girls." The voice had them both turning toward the stairs to find Coal standing there, a grin on his face. "What?"

"How long have you been eavesdropping?" Cyrus shook his head but a smile had the corners of his lips pulled up, too.

"Long enough to hear you apologize for your behavior." Coal strolled toward them until he came up against the back of the sofa, behind her, and reached out to lay his hands on her shoulders. "The girl for you will show up but until then, keep your grease-stained hands off my girl."

"Not all of us can work behind a desk all day." Cyrus shook his head and looked from his brother to her. "I don't know how you can put up working in that office with him all day and then spend all night with him, too. If you ever get tired of his shit, you're always welcome at the house."

"Thanks, but he's not as bad as you make out. Workaholic, yes, but we all have our faults." She reached up and placed her hand over his.

"This workaholic is trying to take off the rest of the day and spend the weekend away with you and no work."

"Well, I'll get out of here." Cyrus rose and glanced back at Coal. "She's good for you, so don't ruin it."

"Thanks, little brother. When this shit has passed, we're going to have to sit down and discuss things, so make a decision."

"Yeah, yeah," Cyrus hollered back as he descended the steps.

"What's that about?" She leaned back, resting her head on the back of the sofa, and looked up at him.

"Come up with me while I pack and I'll explain." He waited for her to come around the sofa before taking her hand and leading them toward the stairs. "Cyrus has always had a talent with old cars. While we've taken on a few over the last several years, mostly for regular clients who want something special, it's been limited. We have an opportunity to expand. A contact of mine owns more than four dozen vintage cars; he came into them when his grandfather died last month. He wants to sell them, but prefers that they go to someone who can bring life back into the cars. They were his grandfather's pride and joy."

"Nearly fifty cars—that's going to be a big project. It also means taking him away from the bikes. Only Cal and Cyrus have the patience and skill to handle the custom paint jobs. Losing him is going to put more work on Cal." He turned to look at her with a raised eyebrow and she added, "Don't look at me. I do pay attention and I've learned a lot about the company in the last few days."

"You have, which is something else I want to discuss with you." He began gathering his thing from the dresser. "Is there room in your bag, or should I grab my own? I hear women pack for a week when they're only going overnight."

"Jerk." She unzipped the bag and sank down on the bed. It was stupid but the idea of them sharing a bag, their things packed side by side, made her stomach tighten with excitement. This was truly happening. "There's room."

"Not all of the cars need a total overhaul. Some run but might need some custom work to live up to our reputation before we can flip them and make a profit. Others are going to take Cyrus' time. But if he can pull it off, he could begin making a name for himself and branch Tanner Cycles in another direction. My heart has always been with motorcycles, same with my brothers—except Cyrus. He's always had the need to be different." A light chuckle rumbled from his chest as she tossed clothes into her bag.

"Here I thought I had your heart; now I find out it belongs to something with two wheels." Keeping her gaze on the floor, she pretended to be hurt by his admission, when she always knew he had a love affair with bikes.

"I'm going to show you that you own my heart. Now let's go." He reached down, took her hand, and pulled her up to stand in front of him. "So fucking beautiful."

"Are you talking about me or your bike?" Unable to keep the grin off her face, she let out a soft chuckle. "Can we take your bike? I want to wrap my legs around you and feel the vibration of the engine between my legs."

"Not tonight, baby. I had to make certain arrangements with Chief Kingsworth in order for him to agree to this and one of them is that I've hired a driver to take us."

"A driver?"

"Yes." He slid his hand up her back, pressing her tight against the front of his body. "I've made a call to the normal car company that I go through when I need a chauffeur and a car should be waiting for us downstairs. Our driver is an undercover police officer. He's there to make sure everything goes as planned. He'll be close by, as the condo is the top floor of a hotel. You have nothing to worry about; you'll be safe."

"I'm not worried about that." She slipped a hand between them, to caress along his crotch. "An hour into the city seems like too long. I want you."

"Baby…" He tangled his fingers in her hair, tugging just enough to cause a little pain to mix with the excitement coursing through her. "I promise it's going to be worth it. We need this."

Now that they had his brothers' blessing, this was just what they needed: a few hours or days without the pressures of family or work. She could forget about Jay and the problem he'd dragged her into. This was time for them to just focus on themselves. Couple time. *We're a couple…*

He pressed his lips to hers, stealing all remaining thoughts, and replacing them with need.

Chapter Eleven

Standing on the condo's balcony overlooking the city of Minneapolis, Sydney felt more relaxed than she had in weeks. Fears of Jay's predicament or his escape from jail to possibly kill her were no longer weighing on her shoulders. She couldn't live with the threat of Jay coming after her hanging over her head forever, but right that moment, she was leaving it to the police to keep her safe and find her brother.

"Syd." Coal slid his arms around her waist, pressing his chest against her back. "You're chilly."

"Umm." She moaned as his lips met the curve of her neck and his warm breath caressed along her skin, sending goosebumps down her arms. "There's something so beautiful about the city from up here."

"I know, it's you." He sucked her earlobe between his teeth. "I can't keep my hands off you."

"Or your mouth, it would seem." She spun around in his arms, so she could look at him. Seeing him standing there, his chest bare and jeans slung low on his hips, made desire spike within her again.

"You're so fucking tempting, it's hard."

She arched her hips into him, grinding her body against the front of him, teasing her hand along his hardness. "It is hard."

"Baby, you keep doing that and we're going to leave room service standing outside the door. Your tiramisu will be the last thing on your mind."

"Dessert then sex, and I promise it will be worth the wait."

"If you stay in just my shirt, we might not make it through dessert before I carry you off to the bedroom."

Circling her arms around his neck, she let out a soft huff. "Those tactics are why that fancy dinner you spoiled me with earlier is in takeout containers in the refrigerator."

"I seem to remember it slightly differently." Sliding his hand under the hem of his dress shirt that she was wearing, he tugged it upward as he caressed along her thigh. "Some vixen spent the entire time enticing me."

"You'll see enticing." She hooked her fingers around the top of his jeans but before she could make her intentions known, a knock at the door interrupted them. "Saved by room service but the longer you make me wait, the more of a tease I'll be."

"I have no doubt." He stepped back from her and headed for the door.

"Coal." She stood in the sliding glass door opening and to prove her point, she licked her lips while slowly unbuttoning another button of the shirt, giving him a better view of her breast. "Hurry back."

"Fuck, baby." Distracted, he pulled open the door, holding it wide for room service to wheel the cart in. That was his first mistake; his second was not looking at the guy wheeling the cart until her jaw went slack with fear.

"Didn't think I'd find you? You thought some fucking cops were going to keep me at bay?" Jay pushed the cart aside, revealing a gun in his hand before kicking the door shut and pointing it at Coal.

"Jay…" She didn't know what to say to him. Fear had overcome her and all she could do was fumble with the button of her shirt, trying to hide

116

from him. She wanted to look at Coal, but tearing her gaze from Jay seemed like the worst thing she could do. If he was there to kill her, she wanted to look him in the eyes. Not because she thought it would weigh on him harder if she forced him to do so, but because she wanted to keep his attention on her. She didn't want Coal to get hurt because of her.

"Jay, come on man. You don't want to do this." Coal's voice was even, even if anger shone through his eyes.

"Like I didn't have to shoot your man in the hallway?" Jay motioned with the gun. "Move! Away from the door, now. You too, Sydney. Both of you in the kitchen. Now!"

Maverick! Move? I can't even feel my legs, let alone force them to walk. Time stood still as she tried to pull herself together. Facing death was something everyone had to do sooner or later. Dying at the hands of Jay was something she was never prepared for. She wanted to face it with confidence, but there was none to be had.

"Come on." Coal wrapped his arm around her waist, bringing her back to the moment.

Things moved in a blur. Jay raised the gun and pulled the trigger but before pain exploded within her, Coal pushed her out of the way. *No!* But it was all over before she could get the word out. The glass door next to where they had been standing exploded, sending glass flying everywhere. As the glass landed on the hardwood floor and the balcony, she realized it sounded louder than the blast from the gun. *A silencer…what if no one knows he's here? We're on our own.*

"Jay…please…."

"Please what?" He waved the gun between her and Coal who had his arm around her waist, keeping her upright. "You're fucking him, aren't you? I fucking trusted you with her and you betrayed me. What the fuck were you thinking, Sydney? He's too old for you." He snapped at Coal before she could even answer his first question.

"You just tried to shoot me! Who's betraying who?" she screamed. "We're family. You've protected me and now you want to kill me. Why?"

"Dad said unless I want to spend the rest of my life in prison like Tim, I can't leave any loose ends." He shook his hand, waving the gun. "Don't fucking change the subject. You're standing there in his fucking shirt, your hair tangled, which leads me to believe you've just fucked him. Did he rape you? Tell me he did and I'll blow his brains all over this place."

"Fuck, Jay!"

"No, Jay!" She shifted her weight and tried to move in front of him, but Coal kept his grip on her, keeping her in place. "A loose end? That's all I am?"

"Shit, Sydney, no. That's why I came for you. We're getting out of here. We're leaving the country. I'm not going down like Tim."

"If you're not guilty—" He raised his eyebrow at her, cutting her off, and chilling the blood that ran through her veins.

"Not guilty." Jay let out a deep laugh, tipping his head back as he did. "I just killed the man Coal had at the elevator. Do you think I'm going to get out of the cage once they've slammed those bars shut around me again? Fuck, no."

"Is there so much rage running through our family that it turns everyone into a murderer? Tim, Dad, and now you." She knew she shouldn't bring it up, but the idea that she could be capable of it ate at her every day. She wanted to believe she was better than that…that she wasn't what her family was, but it weighed on her mind.

"Everyone is capable of murder under the right circumstances. Isn't that true, Coal?" Jay's gaze focused on him. "Did you tell her that you went after Tim? You were prepared to kill him."

Her knees buckled as the past rushed back at her like a freight train barreling down for a deadline. The present was no match as she was transported back to the hospital.

Even after being told no multiple times, she couldn't sit in the waiting room doing nothing. The guard was distracted and all she wanted to do was see him. Her eldest brother lay stretched in the hospital bed, his face flushed from the painkillers coursing through his body, trying to ease his suffering. Two broken legs and countless other injures, she'd overheard the doctors telling her father—but didn't understand.

"Tim…" Her voice broke, and tears swam in her eyes. "Why, Tim?"

The door opened behind her and terrified it could be her father, she climbed on the only chair in the room and pulled the curtain back, hiding herself.

"You fucking bastard!"

Coal? What was he doing there? She wanted to go to him but the anger in his voice kept her frozen in place.

"You killed my parents. Cain might not make it. All because you were too high to keep your car on the road." Something hard hit metal and Tim moaned.

"What the hell? What's the bat for?"

"To bash your fucking brains in. Someone should have done it long ago. But instead of making the world safer, you were behind the wheel tonight. Coming over three fucking lanes of traffic and down the on ramp to slam into two cars, killing the people I love." With every word, Coal's voice rose until he was screaming. "You're the one that deserved to die!"

The door opened and hard soled shoes clicked on the tile. "Hey now, son, you're not supposed to be here." From the voice, she realized it was the officer at the door.

"He murdered my family…my brother…" The anger in Coal's voice mixed with sadness, breaking her heart.

"I know and he's in custody. You can't make him pay like this. Let the courts handle it. You have people who need you. Let's go."

The officer escorted Coal from the room, leaving her hiding behind the curtain, alone with Tim. Murder. She knew things were bad, but Tim was a murderer. Mr. and Mrs. Tanner dead? Cain? Was that why Mom was in a coma? All of this because of Tim?

"Syd." While she was unconscious, Coal had lifted her onto the kitchen counter, so as she came to she was lying looking up at the ceiling, a cool rag pressed to her forehead. His brows were knitted together in concern as he stared down at her. "Easy, baby."

"My dramatic sister. Why the hell did I even come back for you?" Jay's voice seemed far away.

"I never asked you to." Unable to lie on the counter and not face her brother, she started to rise but every muscle in her body felt weak. "Help me sit up?"

"Just to sit. I don't want you getting up yet." Coal wrapped his arm around her shoulder and eased her forward. "Just stay up there, okay?"

With a nod, she glanced toward where she heard the voice and found Jay leaning against the wall into the kitchen, the gun still pointed in their general direction, but not at either of them. "You know what, Jay? I'm done. I'm done with the drama, I'm done questioning if I could ever do what you've done, I'm done with the fear of your enemies. I'm just done with it all. When you went to jail I was terrified, but Coal came and saved me from the dangers you left me in the middle of."

"Yeah, I see he's moved in where he was never wanted." Jay straightened, coming off the wall. "Don't worry about them, I've taken care of it. Their money was never taken by the police; they have it. You're not in danger from them anymore, but you're in danger from him."

"I doubt that." She put her hand over Coal's that was lying on the counter next to her hip.

"Did you even hear me? He tried to kill Tim. He would have if that cop hadn't been there to stop him!" Jay screamed.

"I know." She squeezed his hand. "He told me."

"And you still let him fuck you?"

Fucking wasn't the right word but she let it go because it would only make the situation worse. "Tim got behind the wheel stoned out of his mind, his blood-alcohol level more than twice the legal limit, and plowed into two cars. Two cars that carried people I loved! Mom and Mr. and Mrs. Tanner were killed because of his actions. Mom and Mrs. Tanner suffered extreme pain before their bodies gave in to their injuries. Cain…he'll always have to deal with what happened that night."

"Fuck him. Fuck them. Tim's in prison, on death row—"

"For his own actions." She refused to allow Jay to make Tim out to be the victim in the whole mess. "He killed our mother! How can you have more sympathy for him being in prison than for that fact he stole her life?"

"That whore deserved it!"

She shrugged off Coal's embrace and hopped down from the counter. Forgetting the gun, she stalked toward him. "What did you just call her?"

"Your mother was a whore. Didn't you ever wonder why Dad couldn't even look at you? He never showed any emotion except hatred and disgust toward you."

"Don't." There was a warning within Coal's tone as he came up behind her but she didn't turn around to question him before Jay finished his thought, making her stomach churn.

"You're not his fucking daughter. Your whore of a mother had an affair; she wanted to leave Dad for him but Dad put an end to that. A bloody end to it."

The door busted open and in the blink of an eye, Coal pulled her back, forcing her behind the L-shaped counter and on to her knees. "Get down, baby." If it wasn't for him forcing her to move, she'd still be standing next to Jay, dumbfounded over his announcement.

"Drop the gun! It's over, Jayden."

Gunshots rang out and tears seeped from her eyes as she leaned into Coal's embrace. *Oh god. Please Jay, put the gun down before you get yourself killed.*

Even with a blanket wrapped around Sydney's shoulders, she couldn't shake the chill that rocked her body. When would she get off this rollercoaster ride and have life settle down into a smooth ride again? The last few weeks had been nothing but a horrible ride of ups and downs. The only positive thing that came out of the whole thing was Coal. She pulled the blanket tight around her shoulders and tried to breathe through the flood of memories of her childhood with Jay. Her big brother had always let her hang around him and he put up with her shit; yet, when he'd told her about their mother's affair, he'd stared at her like he didn't even know who she was. They were family, maybe only half-siblings now, but the divide his words caused within her was something she wasn't sure she'd overcome quickly.

"Coal?" A voice hollered from the hallway before others tried to get him to move back. "Get the fuck off me!"

The voice was familiar yet different, making her turn around to see who it was. Fighting against the officers stood a man a head taller than everyone else, his broad shoulders and thick corded muscles strained against the leather of his jacket. His gaze landed on hers and in an instant, she recognized him.

"Coal!" She didn't bother waiting for him to come out of the bedroom where he was speaking with Chief Kingsworth; instead, she rushed toward the commotion at the door. "Get off him."

"This is a crime scene." An officer reached for his cuffs. "Either back up or I'll have to arrest you."

"He's family." She stepped between him and the police. "Now I'm sure you have something better to do than arrest someone who's only here to find out if we're safe."

"You know who I am?" His voice held a hit of surprise as she turned to face him.

"I could never forget you, Cain." She reached out and placed her hand on his chest. "Coal's okay. He's speaking with Chief Kingsworth."

"I was more worried about you." He stood there, his body tight, but he didn't make her remove her hand. "Jay wanted you dead, not Coal."

"I'm not going to ask you again. You need to leave now." The officer reached out to put his hand on Cain.

"Don't fucking touch me." His gaze narrowed at the officer as Cain put his arm around her waist and pulled her to his side so she was no longer standing between him and the officer.

She waited for the violence that appeared to be imminent. She'd witnessed Cain's temper before and she knew that stepping between them could get her hurt. Wondering what was taking Coal so long, she glanced toward the bedroom door just in time to see him strolling toward her, Chief Kingsworth a step behind.

"Get away from my brother!"

"This is a crime scene." The officer took his gaze from Cain for a moment to look back at Coal and when he spotted his boss, his back straightened, waiting for orders. "Sir, he's—"

"He's leaving." Coal made his way toward them, their overnight bag slung over his shoulder. "Come on, Cain. The hotel manager has arranged for us to have a suite. We'll go downstairs and let these officers do their work."

"I just want to go home." She relaxed as Coal's arm slipped around her shoulders.

"Downstairs first and then we'll go anywhere you want." Without giving them a chance to argue, he ushered them toward the elevator. When the doors slid shut, he turned to his brother. "What are you doing here, Cain?"

"I followed Jay but when we got into the city, I lost him. I figured he'd come here first but I couldn't find him so I went to check things out. I overheard the police radio and realized he'd slipped past me so I came to help." Cain stood in the back of the elevator, pressed against the corner, his gaze on the door and every muscle in his body tight.

"Thank you," she whispered, wanting to ease his discomfort.

"I should have arrived earlier. I should have waited here…waited for him to make his move."

They stepped off the elevator and as Coal made his way to the room that was theirs, she paused and waited for Cain. She placed her hand on his arm and as the elevator doors to shut behind them she met his gaze. "Thank you."

"What?" He looked down at her and she took in the man before her.

His long, light brown hair hid the scars that ran along his left side. They started near his ear and covered his arm and also his chest before disappearing into the waistband of his jeans. She remembered when she'd first seen him lying in the hospital bed, half of his body covered in white gauze to protect his burns. Her heart had broken knowing that he'd gotten them while trying to save her mother. Now, he had risked himself again to save her.

"For coming after us." She watched him for a moment, truly expecting him to brush her off, but when he remained silent, she explained. "I know you don't take part in the business, at least not publicly, because of what happened. You stay hidden in your cabin deep in the woods of the property but tonight you left because of me. What was I thinking when I let Coal bring me home with him? I brought this to your doorstep."

"You were thinking about staying alive. You knew you'd be safe here and we'd protect you." He glanced over his shoulder toward Coal. "And did you really think he was going to let you go anywhere else?"

"Syd?" Coal held the door open. "Inside."

"See what I mean...protective." Cain kept his gaze on her but she wasn't sure what to say.

There wasn't a doubt in her mind Coal was protective, but he wasn't just protective of her but also of his brothers, family, and friends. He'd witnessed so much loss in his life—they all had—that he wanted to protect everyone so none of them had to go through such ordeals again.

"Now."

"Come on before you give him a stroke." Cain nodded toward Coal but didn't move away from the elevator doors until she did.

"What's the big deal? It's safe now and we're right here." Even as she complained, she walked toward Coal and the hotel room that had been arranged for them.

"We don't know if what Jay said was the truth and until we do we're not taking any risks." As she approached him, Coal looped his arm around her waist and tugged her against him. "I'm not taking any chances with your safety."

"Then let's go home." She leaned into him. "We're safe there."

"Soon." He ushered her inside and toward the sofa. "Just rest for a minute. I need to speak with Cain."

"Don't leave me."

"We'll be right here." He pulled the blanket that was still around her shoulders tighter. "Just lie back and rest."

She did as he suggested, letting the throw pillow cradle her head, but her thoughts were in too much turmoil to allow her to sleep. Now that the shock of seeing Cain had worn off, her thoughts returned to her brother. They'd rushed him off before she could see him and she wasn't even sure he was still alive. She was only told he'd received life threatening wounds and was in grave condition. What was worse: having him in prison for the rest of his life or death? She'd have said the latter and part of her wondered if that hadn't been what Jay had wanted when he'd opened fire on the police. *I come from a family of murderers.*

Chapter Twelve

What was supposed to be a quiet weekend away for Coal and Sydney had turned out to be full of excitement, though none of it good. He'd wanted the time alone with her to reconnect with her, to show her what she meant to him. Instead, she'd learned heartbreaking things about her mother and him. Now her brother was fighting for his life and Coal wasn't sure how she was handling any of it. She appeared to be shell-shocked but at least she was aware of her surroundings enough to holler for him when Cain showed up.

He tipped his head to his brother, letting him know that he wanted to speak with him alone in the adjoining bedroom. While they wouldn't be out of earshot, it would give them enough privacy that he could determine his brother's mindset. This was the first time in years that Cain had left the family's property, let alone interact with others when he did. If Cain was going to have a breakdown, then Coal needed to get one of his other brothers there. Sydney needed him and he couldn't give them both his full attention at the same time.

Not sure where to start, he stood there for a moment, staring at his brother. The darkness in his eyes and the way he clenched his fist made Coal wonder how close the younger man was to losing it. "Did you call Cay when you left?"

"No." Cain didn't take his gaze from Sydney as he answered, which made Coal uneasy.

"She's not responsible." This was the conversation he didn't want to have with Cain but he knew it had to come out at some point. If Cain resented Sydney because of what had happened, then he needed to know. He would protect her, even if it meant he had to keep her separated from his brother. In the recent past, he'd thought he'd send her on her way if Cain had a hatred for her that was so deep, it put her in danger, but now he wasn't sure he could give her up. If it came down to choosing between his brother and Syd, he knew it wouldn't end well. Either way, he'd lose someone he loved.

"Yes, she is." When Coal adjusted his weight from one foot to the other, Cain glanced at him. "But not in the way you think I mean. She's only eighteen but she's a responsible adult and she's already got your heart. I can tell from the way you look at her. You love her."

"And how do you feel about that?" He wasn't sure what Cain would say or even how he would handle it if his brother despised the woman he loved because of her family's misdeeds. Would Cain be able to put behind him everything that had happened, everything he'd witnessed, and everything he had to overcome, in order to accept Sydney as part of their lives? Or would he be only setting them up for heartbreak and a deep divide between the brothers?

"Are you asking if I have a problem with you and Sydney because her brother murdered our parents and did this to me? Or are you asking because you're terrified I'll go ape shit and fuck up what you have going for you?" Cain glared at Coal for a moment before shaking his head. "I'm not as fucked up as you think I am."

"I don't…I just worry about you." His brother had his issues but Coal wasn't worried about him being a danger to himself or others.

"Then get back to your girl. She needs you more than I do." Cain sat down on the edge of the bed. "Shut the door; I'll wait in here and give you some privacy. Then I'll follow you back home."

"Thanks." Coal stood there a moment before finally nodding and stepping away. "Give me a few minutes and we'll get out of here. She wants to be back home as much as I want her there because I know she'll be safe."

Without wasting another moment, he turned and headed back to the living room. Syd lay curled up in a small ball where he'd left her on the sofa. Her eyes were closed but a gentle shake of her body as she cried let him know she wasn't asleep. He wanted to crush the person who'd made her cry and protect her from all the pain the world had to offer, but he could only do so much. The person who'd brought the tears to her eyes was her own brother, the one who might not even make it through the night, let alone face her again. The cruel world had dealt her yet another devastating blow but he'd make sure it was the last one Jay had the opportunity to deliver.

"Syd." He squatted next to her and took her hand in his. "Baby…"

"I'm awake." Her eyes fluttered open as she tried to hide from him that she had been crying. With her free hand, she wiped the tears away as she sat up. "Are you ready?"

"Soon." He rose to sit next to her on the sofa and pulled her into his arms. "I want to talk to you first."

"About what?"

"Let's start with why you lied to Jay. I've never told you about happened the night of the car accident." He ran his hand down her arm, caressing her softly. "I would have killed Tim that night if the police officer hadn't chosen that moment to come into his room. While I would have regretted hurting you and leaving my brothers behind, I wouldn't have regretted my actions, at least not then. What happened would have been done in anger but he'd have…"

"Deserved it," she supplied when he went silent. "Just because he's my brother…well I guess half-brother…doesn't mean I don't realize that. Your parents were like second parents to me. Your mom is the one who inspired me to stay true to myself. To not let my family force me to do something I didn't want to do. Ever since that heart-to-heart with her, I've done just that."

"How did you know about it?" he pressed when she went off topic.

"I was there." She ran her hand along the front of his chest, tracing each letter of his Tanner Cycles shirt. "No one would tell me anything and I was tired of sitting around the waiting room. When the guard wasn't looking, I was able to sneak inside Tim's hospital room. Then I heard you coming. I didn't know what else to do so I hid behind the curtain and waited."

"You heard me and knew I wanted to kill him, yet you didn't say anything." He stopped rubbing along her back as he waited for her to say something. "Even after all these years, you still never said anything."

"What was there to say?" She tipped her head up toward him. "Did you really think I would just come out and say, 'By the way, Coal, I know you wanted to murder Tim'? Brother or not, I don't think there was a day that went by since that night when I didn't want him dead. His actions— but I'm the one who paid for them. He killed your parents, my mother, and Cain will always have the scars to remind him of what happened. But the greatest loss of all was when you left."

"Oh, baby." He squeezed her tight against him. "We're together now and I'm never letting you go."

"Cain…is he okay?" She glanced over his shoulder toward the bedroom door that he'd shut behind him. "I mean…"

"I know what you mean and he's fine. You talked to him yourself."

"But you were concerned." She turned back to look at him, keeping her voice low. "You told me to stay away from him."

The best way to handle this was to be truthful, so he took hold of her hand, interlacing their fingers. "Cain went through a lot...he's never really been the same since. Before the accident he was the most outgoing and friendly of all of us. He wanted to believe the best in people, that there was more good in the world than bad."

"He was thirteen. We're all like that at that age."

"I wasn't and neither were you. By the time I turned eight, I knew that life was fucked up. Happiness and rainbows didn't exist in our world. It was Uncle Chester's murder that brought that home to me." Huddled together with Cay in his uncle's bedroom closet, he'd wanted to bust the door down and fight for his uncle but he couldn't get out. He'd banged on the door, screaming to get out, but the music was so loud, his uncle's murderer couldn't even hear. That night he hadn't been thinking clearly, and his only excuse was that he'd been only eight years old. His decision to try to get out of the locked closet was made to try to save his uncle; yet, he wasn't just risking his life, but the life of his brother.

"That happened before I was born but Jay told me about it." She scooted onto his lap, straddling him. "Always the hero. You tried to save him."

"I'm no hero. By the time I realized what was happening, I couldn't have saved my uncle, but I could have gotten both Cay and me killed." Uncle Chester had stepped into a fight the night before, saving a waitress at the bar he was a bouncer at from her abusive ex-husband whom she had a restraining order against. He'd never considered it would end with both him and the woman dead within twenty-four hours. Even if he had, he'd have still done it. That was the kind of man Uncle Chester had been.

"You've always been and always will be my hero." She looped her arms around his neck, bringing their faces close. "I love you, Coal."

"I love you too, and when we get home, I'm going to show you how much." He trailed teasing fingers along the hem of the shirt she was still wearing. "First, do you want me to see if I can get you in to see Jay before we head back to Davenport?"

He didn't like the idea of his woman being near someone who had hurt her like he had only hours before—someone who had instilled so much fear into her. It had taken more self-control than he'd thought he possessed not to beat the fuck out of Jay when he'd pointed a gun at her. If for one moment he thought Jay would have actually shot his sister, he'd have killed the bastard where he stood, but it wasn't in Jay. He might be a murderer but he wouldn't kill Sydney; she was family and to him that mattered, at least a little bit.

"Baby?" he pressed when she remained silent.

"No." She leaned away from him, the blanket falling off her shoulders. "I feel horrible about it but no. He might be dying but I can't do it. I know he said he came back for me so we could leave the country but if I refused to go, he'd have killed me. Family doesn't mean anything to him. He'd have done what he needed to do to save his own ass."

"I'd have never let that happen." He reached up to tangle his fingers in her hair. "You know that, don't you, baby?"

"I know." She nodded. "Maverick! Shit, I forgot. Is he…" The words died in her throat as her eyes widened.

"It's okay, baby. He's okay. Shot but alive, though his attitude is pretty unpleasant from what I've been told. They're keeping him in the hospital overnight for observation due to the blood loss, and Cay will pick him up in the morning."

"Then let's go home and forget about this whole mess." She slipped off his lap and rose to stand in front of the sofa.

"Home sounds good."

She dropped the blanket onto the armrest and paused, her gaze not meeting his. "I mean unless you don't want me to go back to your place...I can, um...find somewhere..."

"Uncertainty has you questioning things." He took hold of her hand that was hovering over the blanket. "Listen to me, Syd. I love you and want you with me always. It's our home now. If you don't like the apartment above the shop, we'll build a home that is all ours on the property. I don't care as long as I have you in my life."

"I just thought now that everything is over you might not want me staying with you."

"Fuck that." He rose off the sofa and came to stand in front of her. "The actions of your jackass brother brought us together but there's no way I'm letting you go now. I've waited too long for you."

"Then let's stop waiting and start living. There's nothing over our heads anymore. Dad and Tim are in prison, and Jay will be joining them if he survives. I'm alone now."

Hearing the sadness in her voice, he lopped his arm around her. "You're never alone. You've got me, my brothers, Maverick, Tank, and more people than you've had the chance to meet yet. We're family and you're part of that."

"I've always had you."

"Yes, baby, you did; you just didn't know it." He slid his hand along the length of her body. "Now get some pants on so we can go home. I'll call for the car and let Cain know we're heading out."

He waited until she went to their overnight bag before he walked toward the door to the adjoining bedroom. With Sydney seeming to be doing better than she had been, he needed to shift his attention to his brother for a moment. Cain could tell him anything he wanted but was it the truth? He wasn't sure. Only time would tell. At least, once they were back at the family's compound, he could rely on Cay to help watch over Cain. The next few days or even weeks would be a great indicator of how Cain would accept Sydney into their lives. While their interactions so far had been positive, he wasn't completely convinced that her presence wouldn't bring back memories of the car accident or the days following the horrific events. He could only hope that one day his brother would find the love that he had with Syd and he'd be able to put the past behind him, once and for all.

 Chapter Thirteen

The romantic weekend Coal had planned to spend with Sydney hadn't worked out and even once they arrived back home, it proved impossible for them to sit around and do nothing. Without news of her brother's condition, Syd was restless but she refused to allow him to inquire about his status. They'd wait until Chief Kingsworth or one of the others called her with an update. It had been less than twelve hours since the incident and she didn't want to pester them. Trying to get her mind off things, they sat in his office working. She was still reorganizing the books to her liking and he was trying to focus on the orders in front of him.

"Let's get out of here."

"Huh?" Without looking up at him, she reached up to grab the pen she'd stuck in her ponytail.

"We need to go shopping." He shut the lid to his laptop and set it aside. "Shuffling back and forth between the desk and sofa isn't working. If we're going to work together and share this office, then we need to refurnish it. I could have the guys clean out the other office but I'd rather keep you close by."

"Afraid someone else will steal me away?" She glanced up at him as her fingers pounded away at the keyboard. "You know I might just get a better offer and take them up on it."

"A better offer than me? I doubt that." He shot her a cocky grin. "Seriously, Syd."

"So you want this long term? I mean me working with you…for you."

"Do you have another tempting offer?" He rose from the sofa and went to lean against the desk next to her.

"Maybe." She leaned back in the leather office chair, watching him with a playful gleam in her eyes. "After all, who wants to work for a workaholic?"

"Pot meet kettle."

"Huh?" Her eyebrows knitted together.

"Since you arrived, you've been as much of a workaholic as I am and don't give me that shit about you not having anything else to do."

"Have you seen the state of your books?" She reached forward, grabbing the paper copy of his books. "Who keeps physical copies like this? I feel like I've fallen into the nineties again where people didn't trust computers. Your life would have been less complicated if you'd have set it up properly using an accounting program to begin with. It would make calculations for you, giving you everything you need without all the work."

"Simple for you but that system and I have had our issues, until I threw in the towel. *Old* people like me don't get along as well with computers as you younglings." He winked at her. "That's why I need you." Hell, even if she hadn't made running Tanner Cycles easier, it wouldn't change things. He wanted her in every way.

"You're not old and you could do it with training. I took an accounting class in my last year of high school, which is why I know this program, so don't give me that old crap."

"Testy baby? Come here, let me relieve your stress." He hooked his foot on the bottom of the chair and scooted her closer to him. "I was planning on waiting to have you on the desk until after we got new furniture, but I think it would be a fitting way to send this one off."

"Yeah, I'm testy when you bring up our age difference. It reminds me of what Jay said." She rose out of the chair before she pushed it away so she was standing in front of him, not yet touching, but close enough that if either of them moved, they'd brush against one another. "When I look at you, I don't see an age difference. To me you're just the man I love; age never comes into play. Do others look at us and see an age difference? Do they think I'm only with you because you're rich? Because, like age, money has never played into it. You know that, right?"

"Syd." He reached out and placed his hands on her hips, his thumb teasing under the hem of her shirt until he was touching skin. "I know, baby. My comment about age was senseless and I apologize. Your age played a part in me wanting to deny my attraction to you. I wanted you to have everything you wanted and besides being a workaholic, I'm set in my ways. But now I don't think of an age difference; you are my girl. Young and beautiful or old and gray, you'll always be my girl."

"Gray!" Her mouth dropped open as if she was stunned but a glint of amusement danced in her eyes.

"One day far in the future you will have gray hair but it will happen long after it happens to me. Hell, I'm sure, if you look closely, you'll see my brothers have already given me some."

"You avoided part of my question. Do you think people look at us and only see the age difference or think I'm only with you for your money?" The look in her eyes warned him she wasn't going to give up until she got an answer. Even if she heard what she feared, she'd rather he gave an honest answer instead of sidestepping the question altogether.

"Fuck everyone else. We're happy and that's what matters." He pulled her closer to him. "There's always going to be some asshole with a comment. Someone who doesn't want others to be happy because they're miserable. But we're not going to let that divide us. Are we?"

"What about Cay and Cal? Are they okay with it? Cain seemed so but is he, really? Cyrus came around so I'm not worried about him. What about the rest of the people who mean something to you? Tank? Maverick? Hell, Maverick could have been killed if Jay hadn't been preoccupied that night, and it's all because of me."

"No, Syd. Maverick was shot because Jay knew he would stop him from gaining access to you and the authorities would be notified. He didn't want to end up back behind bars, looking at life in prison. Now he's only made things worse for himself. He added multiple charges, including attempted murder on a police officer. The judge is going to throw the book at him."

"If he survives." Her voice was barely above a whisper as she leaned into his chest.

"Do you want to call to find out about his status?" he offered again so she knew that the offer was still on the table.

"I don't want to see him."

"But you want to know if he's okay." He nodded, reading between the lines. "How about this: while you get ready for our shopping trip, I'll make the call. Give me ten minutes and we'll go."

"Shopping." She grinned. "Okay, but before we send this desk off, I want you to make love to me on it. Seems only fitting since this is where I captured your heart. Then, once the new ones arrive, we'll have to do it all over again to make sure I keep your heart."

"Syd, my sweet girl, my heart has and will always belong to you." He pressed his lips to hers in a quick kiss because if he did anything more, he'd have her naked on the desk and their shopping trip would be forgotten.

"Now go on before I forget our plans and get you naked, screaming my name before you can even blink."

"That sounds like an even better way to spend the afternoon." Her words didn't match her actions as she stepped back from him and headed for the stairs. "This shopping trip better be more exciting than getting fucked on the desk; otherwise, you might end up with blue balls tonight."

"I'll make the wait worth it." He sat down in the leather office chair she'd vacated only moments before and reached for the phone. He waited until he heard her reach the top of the stairs before he turned his attention to the phone in his hand and called Chief Kingsworth. While Jay wasn't in the Davenports Police custody any longer, Chief Kingsworth would know who to contact to determine his status.

Jay was an asshole and his will to live was strong; it had to be since he'd risked so much to break out of jail. He only hoped for Sydney's sake that his will to live was still there. It would be better for her to be able to see her brother in prison, with the rest of her family, than in a wooden box six feet under. In prison she could make her peace with him; if he was dead she'd never find closure.

The shopping trip was unlike any others Sydney had gone on before. It hadn't been enough for Coal to just purchase furniture; he had forced her to shop for herself. Her thoughts had been filled with questions about Jay; though Coal had tried, they hadn't been able to get an update on his condition, so they were waiting for someone to call them back. To get her mind off things, he had forced her to go clothes shopping. While she hadn't been in the mood to look for outfits, she found it to be the perfect distraction.

As they loaded the last of the bags into the back of his SUV, his words played through her thoughts again. *You're my assistant now; you need clothes that fit your new position. As much as I love the way your jeans hug your curves like a second skin, you'll need dresses and business suits. If I must play the part, then so do you. There's a fundraiser coming up in two weeks and I want you on my arm. We'll find you something elegant and sexy. Every head will turn when you walk into the room. Everyone will be envious you're mine.'*

She waited until they were back in the SUV, with Coal driving them home before she turned to him. "What did you mean earlier when you said if you have to play the part so do I? Don't you like the work you do?"

"I love Tanner Cycles almost as much as I love being on my bike. It's just the business side of things I hadn't completely understood when I was getting involved in this. The jeans and t-shirts I prefer have to be replaced with business suits, or worse, tuxedos. I miss working in the shop next to my brothers every day but more than that, I miss taking off on my bike whenever I feel the need."

"Why don't you? I mean I understand business gets in the way and you're a workaholic so you don't know when to quit, but surely you could find a balance. I can't do anything about the suits and tuxedos. After all, I did see your schedule and the commitments you have on the books are numerous. But let me handle more of the office stuff and you could get down there with your brothers once in a while. As for taking a ride on your bike, I've been asking you. It's been too long since I've been on the back of a motorcycle. I miss the way the wind slides over my body and the freedom."

"There are a few hours of daylight left. Let's get home and go for a short ride. After spending hours shopping, it will be the perfect way to end the day." He accelerated, passing a slower car that was in the way.

"What about the other part? You know I could handle the office work and you could work in the shop. That's why you started Tanner Cycles in the first place, so why not get back to your roots? It's not like I'm any help down there. I don't know anything about bikes. Hell, I barely know how to change a tire on a car."

"What was that you said earlier?" He glanced at her before turning back to the road. "That's right, it's teachable. I could teach you anything you want to know about a bike and most things about a car, but for older models you might need to spend some time with Cyrus. He's into restoring old cars and has the patience for it. I don't; I'd rather spend my time doing other things, like making love to you."

"We better get back to the house. I want to make love on the desk before we tear the office apart for the new furniture arrival tomorrow." She reached over to place her hand on his thigh. "The office is going to be first class but are you sure either of us is going to get any work done sharing that space? Maybe we should clean out the space you previously used for your assistants. I'm sure we could put the parts stored in there somewhere else."

"Are you trying to get away from me?" His voice was strained as his gaze stayed focused on the road.

"Never." She squeezed his thigh. "I like the idea of our desks being across from each other and every time I look up, I'll see you there across from me. I think that's the best view any girl could ask for."

"Plus, I thought you were trying to convince me to get into the shop more. Which means you'd have the office to yourself sometimes anyways."

"If that's what you enjoy then why not? I can handle the office—placing orders, accounting, scheduling, and everything else. Now that I'm getting the books just as I want them, there's no way I'm letting you anywhere near them." A semi truck passed next to them, making her look up at it. There was nothing different about it but for some reason it caught her attention. Growing up, Jay had always said he was going to be a trucker, because he wanted to see the country and that was the only way to do it. Before he came to Minnesota after her, he hadn't even left the state of Pennsylvania except to travel to Ohio on rare occasions when drugs needed to be transferred. Was he still in Minnesota? She wasn't sure but suspected he would be because of his grave condition.

"Syd." He caressed her hand that was resting on his leg, popping her thoughts like a bubble. "You get to decide: a ride on the bike or office sex?"

"Can't I have both?" She teased her fingers along the inside of his thigh, working upwards, closer to his cock. "You know you want both."

"Fuck, baby, you're a tease." As he took the exit that would lead them into Davenport, he arched his hips forward—she wasn't sure if it was to give her a better angle or to readjust himself. Either way, it urged her on, enjoying the feel of him hardening under the faintest touch. "Two minutes and we'll be home."

She didn't want to wait; she wanted him now but the side of the road in the middle of Davenport just wouldn't do. The chances of them getting caught were too high and that was not the kind of publicity Tanner Cycles needed. She undid the top button of his jeans as he turned onto the dirt road that led back to the family's property.

"Wait." He took hold of her hand but it was the stillness of his body that caught her attention.

"What?" Glancing up at him, she found his facial features had hardened, his eyes had turned darker, and the need that had been there moments before was gone. Rather, he stared out the front window, watching something. As she followed his line of sight, she realized what had stopped him.

Her heart beat frantically against her ribs and her chest tightened, making it harder to get air into her lungs. Two police cars near the main gate of the property sent fear rushing through her. Cay and Cyrus were speaking with one of the officers, but she couldn't make out who the other man was. "Coal?"

"It's okay, baby." He squeezed her hand but wouldn't meet her gaze as he pulled the SUV to a stop a few feet from the police cruisers. "Stay here. I'll find out what's going on."

"I'm coming with you." She opened her door before he put the SUV in park and watched as the men's attention turned toward them. Even Cyrus who was always easygoing couldn't quite meet her gaze. His shoulders drooped as if he had the weight of the world on them. Terrible thoughts of losing Coal rushed through her mind. Could Jay have said something to the police that would have sent them there to arrest Coal? Even if Jay disagreed with their relationship, she was eighteen, making her legal. There was still the possibility Jay could have accused Coal of something else. *I'll kill him for this.*

Meeting Coal at the front of the SUV, he slipped his hand into hers and whispered something to her that she didn't catch because of her overwhelming thoughts. The men moved away from the fence, with Cyrus being the last to move. The way he lingered behind warned her he didn't want to be there for this but felt he had to. The youngest of the Tanner brothers seemed to be the most emotional but whatever had disturbed him was bleeding off on Cay as well. When Cay looked at her, there was only sadness peeking through his pale blue eyes.

"Mr. Tanner, Ms. Manor, if I may have a few minutes of your time."

Tearing her gaze from Cay and Cyrus, she took in the man in uniform and recognized him as Chief Kingsworth. If she had taken the time to look at him before, she'd have known him immediately from his height and the way he held himself. He was the law in Davenport, and his six-foot-seven frame made sure everyone realized it.

"Chief Kingsworth, I called you earlier but you didn't need to make a special trip out here. A call would have been sufficient." Coal's voice was light as if he wasn't worried about the chief's sudden appearance, but the stiffness in his body let her know otherwise.

"The news I'm about to deliver is better handled in person if possible than over the telephone." He glanced at her before looking back at Coal. "We should do this inside."

"What's going on?" she demanded. "I'm not going anywhere until you tell me what's happening."

"Shh, baby." Coal let go of her hand and wrapped his arm around her shoulders, drawing her against his body.

"Chief Kingsworth is right. We should go inside. It's about…" Cay moved to the chief's side, his gaze more on Coal than on her, as if he was trying to silently communicate with his brother.

"She's already upset, so just say what needs to be said."

"Tell me!" Her voice was louder than she'd planned but anger and fear were controlling her. *Please don't be here to arrest Coal. Not my Coal!*

Chief Kingsworth didn't look pleased but he nodded. "The doctors have done everything they can for Jayden but his chance of survival is unlikely. He needs to have surgery to repair the damage one of the bullets has caused to his heart. That organ is the most damaged but his whole body is shutting down. He's suffering with multiple internal injuries, leaving the doctors to decide which needs to be a priority. Without the surgery, he'll die, but the chance of surviving the procedure is less than ten percent."

"You need my permission for the surgery." Even to her own ears, her voice sounded calm—while inside she was falling apart. Her legs felt weak and if it wasn't for Coal's arm around her waist, she wasn't sure she'd still be in an upright position.

"That and I've made arrangements for you to see him if you wish. It could be your last chance."

Her vision swam as she realized her brother was going to die. That was enough to have her crumbling toward the ground as her legs gave out from under her but Coal's arm tightened around her. *I'd rather be dead than in prison.* Was it selfish that she'd rather see him alive? Maybe, but even after everything he'd done, she couldn't wish her brother dead. "I want to see him."

Chapter Fourteen

Since the night of her mother's accident, Sydney hated hospitals. They only served as a reminder of the life and love that had been ripped away from her. Tim had robbed her of her mother, as well as Mr. and Mrs. Tanner, and eventually, the Tanner brothers. With her mother gone, Dad had become more distant and now she knew why. Everything she loved she'd lost that night, the only exception being Jay. Now she was standing in another hospital room about to lose another piece of herself.

Jay was dying and while Chief Kingsworth had tried to make the surgery seem like a possibility of saving his life, the doctors caring for him didn't seem to have the same belief. The surgery was Jay's only hope, the doctors had warned her countless times that his survival was unlikely. Her heart was breaking as she tried to brace herself for losing him.

With tears rolling down her face, she stood by his bed, his hand in hers. She wanted to rant and rave about what had happened, to curse him for breaking out of jail and for raising a gun on police officers, but she didn't. He couldn't hear her and while it might make her feel better for the moment, it wouldn't give her the peace she craved.

"Come on, Syd, sit down." Coal pushed a hard metal chair up behind her so she could sit next to the bed. "You're too pale. I don't want you passing out. Sit...please."

She did as he'd asked partially because she didn't have the strength to fight him and partially because she felt as though she would topple over. Just being in this place overwhelmed her and made her feel lightheaded. Since the car accident, hospitals only meant one thing to her—death. In her mind, it didn't matter some sick people came there, got better, and went home. It didn't matter that new life was born in the maternity ward every day. All she could focus on was the loss that had transpired in a hospital very similar to the one she stood in.

A soft moan came from Jay and he tried to move his arm that was handcuffed to the bed. Though he wasn't in any condition to walk out of there, the police were not taking any chances. She tipped her head back to look up at Coal.

"The officers he…" the words failed her. Knowing her brother had shot two police officers and actually saying the words aloud were two different things.

"They're alive." He squeezed her shoulder. "One will be discharged today and the other was in surgery this morning when I called Chief Kingsworth. That's why he wasn't in the office."

"Will he live?" She wasn't sure she wanted to know the answer but she couldn't stop herself from asking the question. The idea that her brother might have killed a law enforcement agent made her sick.

"If the surgery is successful."

"Sy…Sydn…" Jay's voice was rough and full of pain but he knew she was there.

"I'm here, Jay. I'm here." She squeezed his hand. "It's okay. Don't talk."

"Coal?"

"He's here." She wasn't sure if she should be telling Jay that or not. "Don't worry about a thing. It's going to be okay."

"I'm dying."

Was she supposed to argue with him? Was she supposed to tell him the surgery would fix everything? If she was, she knew she couldn't do it. Lying to someone wouldn't make anything better and she wasn't sure it would make him fight to live, either. The idea of her brother dying felt like a knife stabbing her through her heart.

"It's okay…it's better than…prison." His voice was ragged and breathy. The pain swam in his eyes as he opened them to look at her. "Don't cry."

"Don't die on me and I won't have to." She lowered the bed rail so she could scoot closer to him. "Fight, Jay. Fight to live. You're all I have left."

"Bullshit." He tipped his chin toward Coal who was still standing behind her. "You've got him. He went behind my back and fucked you. Our friendship meant nothing to him when it came to claiming you—that better mean he fucking loves you."

"Jay—" She started to defend what happened between them but Coal's hand tightened on her shoulder.

"You have nothing to worry about. I do love her and she will be taken care of no matter what happens." She noticed that Coal didn't try to defend their friendship but asking about it now would waste what little time she had with her brother.

"If I make it through this…" Jay coughed, sending blood dripping from his lip.

She grabbed a tissue from the box by the bed and wiped up the bright red blood; all the while her mind screamed for the doctor to get there, to perform the surgery and save her brother. "Don't talk, just rest."

"Listen to me." With his free hand, he caught hold of her arm, stopping her from wiping away the remaining blood. "I'll take a deal. I

149

won't put you through the stress of having to testify against me. If I die…remember the good times we shared. I should have never told you about…Mom's affair. She was a good woman. She wanted more than Dad could give her. There's no shame to that."

"I love you, Jay." She wanted to wrap her arms around him but with his injuries and the cords from the medical equipment, she couldn't; instead, she leaned down and pressed a gentle kiss to his cheek. "You're my big brother; our good memories far exceed any bad ones. You kept me safe through the years—for that I'll always be thankful."

"I've been a shit to you." He squeezed her arm, just above the elbow. "Don't deny it. This last year I could feel the divide between us. I didn't know what else to do but try to force you into the so-called family business."

"Don't worry about it." She blinked, trying to keep the tears at bay. "It's going to be okay."

"I know you will be." He looked past her toward Coal. "You take good care of her. Make her happy. She deserves it."

"You have my word." Coal slipped an arm around her waist as he came to stand closer behind her. "I love her and I hope with time you can accept this."

Before Jay could respond, his body shook with another coughing fit and machines beeped. "Jay!" she screamed as his eyes rolled back in his head and his body started to seize. "No! Jay…please…"

"Someone. We need help in here! Doctor!" Coal hollered and she realized he wasn't behind her, but at the door, shouting down the hallway.

"Don't you dare die on me. Do you hear me Jay?" Tears rolled down her face as she held the tissue to his mouth, trying to catch the blood that was seeping out from between his lips.

Hands wrapped around her arms, pulling her back from the bed. "Come on, Syd. Let them do their work."

She hadn't realized the nurses had joined them, or even the man in a white coat who she had spoken with earlier. She fought through the fear surrounding her thoughts and tried to remember the doctor's name, but it was as if a hole had been drilled in her memories. Coal pulled her away from the bed, toward the back wall of the hospital room so they were out of the way of the medical staff.

"Get them out of here." The doctor tipped his head to the nurse.

"Come on, Syd." Coal wrapped his arm around her shoulder and ushered her toward the door. "We have to let them do their work. There's nothing we can do for him now."

"He's right, Ms. Manor." The young nurse looked from Coal to Sydney. "Let me take you to the family waiting room and someone will come speak with you shortly."

"We can find it. Help the doctor." Coal pulled her out the room before the nurse could argue, leading her quickly passed the officer at the door and down the hallway before she could protest.

He seemed to understand that she wouldn't want to fall apart in front of so many witnesses, even if she hadn't managed to decide that for herself. Mentally she was a mess and she was surprised she could even keep her feet under her as they made their way to the waiting room. Jay had done some horrible things in his life but he was still her family and the idea of him dying broke her heart.

After everything that had happened, she hadn't wanted to see him and hadn't even been sure she'd have visited him in prison, but she didn't want him dead. Even thinking about possibly visiting Jay in prison made her stumble as Coal led her through the door to the waiting room. The pale green walls and worn out sofas made her want to run. How many people had sat in this very room, waiting to find out if their loved ones were going to make it? How many had received the devastating news that they had died? Would she be handed that same news shortly?

They made their way to the sofa closest to the small beverage stand and he helped her sit down on it before turning toward the coffee pot. Even in the haze of emotions, she was thankful the room was empty. The last thing she wanted was people watching her, wondering what her story was.

"I've never visited Tim...I refused to visit him. Once Dad tried to force me but that was the one thing Jay had stood up to him about and he never brought it up again."

"Drink this." He pressed a warm mug of coffee into her hand. "If they had something stronger I'd have put it in there but it's a hospital and they tend to frown on alcohol use in moments like this. I don't want to leave you alone to find someone to get liquor, either."

"I don't want..." She stopped because at that moment a strong drink sounded perfect. Short term relief but still relief for the moment. The problems, grief, and sorrow would all still be there whenever the alcohol wore off but a moment of peace was all she needed. Yet, she went ahead and took a sip of the coffee because she didn't want him to go anywhere.

The warm liquid helped to center her and keep her focused on the moment. "Even once Dad went to prison, I wouldn't go to see him. I didn't want to remember him like that; at least, that's what I told myself. In truth, the moment he was convicted, I disconnected myself from him. I was embarrassed by the fact he was my father...well, at least at the time I thought he was. With Tim, I was filled with hatred over what he'd done. To this day, I can't get past it. I can't look at a picture of him without feeling the rage return. I cut him off and refused to consider him. But even when I knew Jay had committed murder and after everything else he'd put me through, I couldn't disconnect myself from him. He was all I've had for so many years. When Mom died and you left, we got closer. The last year or so has been rough; he's been under more stress. Instead of talking to me about it, he shut me out. Even after everything that's happened, I knew I would go see him in prison. I couldn't just remove myself from him, even after his actions could have cost me my life. Now he's…" She couldn't say the word *dying*, even if she knew that's what was happening.

"You were always closer to Jay than to Tim, so it was easier for you to close Tim off without the loss you'd suffer now. You dealt with the shit life dished out to you the best way you could. There was nothing wrong with cutting Tim or your father off. They made their choices and you had to do what was best for you." He sat down on the sofa next to her, his hand on her knee. "I went to see Tim once."

"When?" She jerked, forcing the coffee to slosh around in the cup, and looked at him. "You never said anything about it."

"It was almost two years ago, just after Cain turned eighteen. Cain needed to face him to gain closure over what happened but it didn't help. Tim doesn't take responsibility for his actions. He still blames the accident on drugs and alcohol. He's cocky as if he's done no wrong and now that Pennsylvania has put a stay on the death penalty, he feels he's got a reprieve. He'll spend the rest of his life behind bars but he's still alive, unlike your mom and my parents. He doesn't have to face the world with the burns that serve as daily reminders to Cain."

"Tim would never take blame for anything he did. I'm not surprised he hasn't changed; if anything, from what Jay told me, prison has made Tim harder. I still don't understand how Dad and Jay had any contact. Dad's in prison in Waynesburg, an hour away from where Jay was held in the Pittsburgh jail waiting trail."

"There are always ways to get a message to someone if you need to but it's possible Jay and your father spoke about not leaving a witness behind before he was arrested. The visits were regular between them, making it easy for him to confide in your father after the murder but before he was arrested. But Jay wasn't going to kill you."

She wrapped her hands around the coffee mug and shook her head. "He would have if I hadn't gone with him. There might be a bond between us but his need for self-preservation would outweigh our family ties. He'd kill me if it meant he might walk away from the murder charges. He knows he's going down on drug charges, but the sentence would be lighter and he'd have the possibility of being a free man within a few years."

"I want to argue that but I can't." There was a softness to his voice that had her glancing over at him. "I know that look. You expected me to argue with you but how can I when I'm not convinced he wouldn't have tried to kill you? I brought Maverick in because of his military training, thinking he'd be able to keep you safe. If he hadn't been speaking with the officer who traveled with us to the condo, Jay would have never got the drop on us. When he stepped in, I cursed myself for not checking. I risked your safety because I was relaxed and trusted the men outside the door. He could have killed them and still made it to us but I didn't even bother to check the peephole before opening the door. That was careless of me and I put you in danger because of it."

"Coal." She set the coffee aside and turned to him. "You protected me; nothing about that was careless. If our shields were down, it was because we were both relaxed and trusted that we were safe. He hadn't made his move and part of me thought he'd find someplace where he could lie low and not get caught. I hadn't considered him leaving the country. I realize now I didn't consider that option because it would have been difficult and too expensive. Jay always took the easy way out and he spent the money he made as fast as it came in. Living beyond our means was one of the reasons the cops started to suspect him picking up things from my father."

"Ms. Manor."

The sound of her name being called forced her to look away from Coal, only to find the doctor coming toward them. He wouldn't meet her gaze and before he even opened his mouth, she knew her brother was gone. "No. Get back in there and save him." Tears swam in her eyes and her chest tightened.

"I'm sorry. We did everything we could."

"You told me he needed surgery. That it was his only chance. Why did you wait? I was sitting by his bedside for over an hour. He should have been taken for surgery immediately!" With every word, her voice grew louder until she was screaming at him. "You did this. He lost his chance because you caused a delay in his care."

"Syd." Coal wrapped his arms around her, holding her tighter as she lashed out at the only person she could.

"Ms. Manor, I believe my colleague explained that if the surgery had any chance of being successful, there was only one person who could do it. He was two hours away and had just arrived at the hospital when Mr. Manor's condition began to deteriorate." He glanced at Coal. "Mr. Tanner saw me in the hallway with another doctor when he hollered for help. That was Doctor Mizanin, the doctor we've been waiting for. We were on our way to examine Mr. Manor and have him prepared for surgery. I assure you there was no delay in his treatment and that we were doing everything we could for your brother."

"I have to see him."

"Are you sure, Syd?" Coal rubbed up and down her arm. "You don't need to see him like that. He wants you to remember the good times."

"I need to…" She wasn't sure why but she had to see him, had to know for sure he was dead. Maybe it was all the lies she had been told her whole life, but she needed confirmation on this, to know for sure he was truly dead. No matter the reason, she wouldn't be talked out of it.

"Very well, I'll let the nurses know." The doctor took a step back before pausing. "I'm sorry for your loss."

Sorry, as if that changes anything. Even inside her own thoughts, she realized she was being harsh. It wasn't the doctors' fault that Jay was dead. He'd brought this on himself the moment he opened fire on law enforcement. Some might even say he deserved what he got but even after everything he did, he was her brother and she couldn't wish him dead. *I already miss you, Jay.*

Chapter Fifteen

Days passed and finally, the small, intimate affair to honor Jay's life was behind Sydney but the loss of her brother remained like a hole in her chest. Coal and his brothers had been there every step of the journey for her, comforting her in ways she had never experienced or expected. They had taken her into their fold and in a way, they had become her family. She was in love with Coal and they meant everything to him; therefore, they meant a lot to her, too.

When she'd first arrived, Coal had told her he wanted her to stay away from Cain. He hadn't been sure how his brother would react to her presence and considered he might see her as a reminder of the past. No one had expected he would open up to her the way he had. He had followed them to Minneapolis because he'd spotted Jay on their tail and wanted to make sure she was safe. The connection between them grew stronger over the days that followed that terrible night. He had been the one she had been able to confide in and even when she didn't feel like talking, he seemed to know exactly what she needed to say.

While Cain had rarely left his cabin in the woods, he had done just that for her—not once, but twice. To have him there for her meant everything to her. Words couldn't express what that simple gesture meant to her.

She leaned back against the sofa and let her eyes fall shut. Instantly, her thoughts drifted back to the small memorial service Coal had put together. It wasn't much because no one knew Jay there in Davenport. Chief Kingsworth and some of the other officers from the Davensport Police Department came to show their support. Even the two officers that had been shot by Jay had made an appearance; he wanted to let her know he had no hard feelings toward her, which was something that had bothered her. Jay had come to Minnesota after her, involving the local and state law enforcement agencies. Knowing one of them had ended up hurt because of her made her feel guilty, even though she hadn't been the one who'd pulled the trigger.

The most memorable aspect of the memorial service had been Cain's presence. He had come to support her, although he had been withdrawn from the others, hovering in the back until he could get a moment of her time. His words were brief but he had made an appearance and made sure she knew he was thinking of her. To some it was a simple gesture but for him, it signified a huge step and this meant more to her than anything else.

"Syd?" Coal's voice was low, letting her know he was hoping she had finally fallen asleep and he wasn't about to wake her.

"I'm awake." Opening her eyes, she found him standing a few feet away, still in his suit from earlier but his tie had been loosened as if he could no longer stand the noose around his neck. "I thought you had a business call you had to take."

"Cay's handling it." He sat down next to her, drawing her into his arms. "You're more important. Always Syd, always."

"I'm fine." She leaned into his embrace and rested her head on his chest. "It's been a rough few days but things are bound to get easier. Tomorrow we leave for my first business trip as your assistant. I should be excited about it."

"About that, Cay offered to go in my place."

"Why?" She tipped her head up toward him so she could see him. "Because of me?"

"Syd—"

"No, Coal. You've already put too much on hold for me. Your brothers have stepped up to help, doing things you would normally do on top of their own work. I appreciate it because it gave us time together and I needed that. But enough is enough. Getting back to work will help me move forward. But there's something else I must do."

"Name it."

"I have to go to Waynesburg, Pennsylvania. I need to see my father and find out the truth."

"He might not discuss it." He rubbed small circles down the length of her back. "There's no statute of limitation on murder. If he admits he killed your biological father, he could face charges for it if enough evidence is gathered. As it stands, he could be released from prison before he dies. Unlikely, but it's possible. Another murder charge and that possibility disappears."

"Then we'll see Tim. He's on death row in the same supermax security prison." She watched him for a moment before adding, "I have to at least try."

He seemed to consider it for a moment before he nodded. "I understand the need to know the truth but there might be another option. If I can get you the answers without involving your father or Tim, would that satisfy you?"

"How? Because if I could have thought of another option I wouldn't be considering visiting my father. He's the one who planted the idea in Jay's head that he needed to kill me before I could testify against him. What kind of father does that?"

"Maverick's mother." He paused, allowing her a moment to let that sink in. "I never considered the possibility that your mother had an affair but Jay's announcement made things click. She raised Maverick alone after her husband abandoned her and to supplement her income, she rented out the basement apartment."

"I don't understand."

"Anthony Brown rented the apartment. I was there a lot hanging out with Maverick. He lived closer to me so I would stop by his house and we'd head over to Jay's together. It wasn't until Jay mentioned an affair that I remembered seeing your mother there a lot." His hand stilled at the center of her back and his gaze found hers. "Anthony went missing a month after you were born. If I remember what I overheard, the police believed he was murdered. I was only ten at the time so I might not be remembering things correctly, but I believe they found blood in the apartment."

"Can you call her and see what she remembers? If she knows anything?"

"If your mother confided in anyone, it would have been her. They were good friends. Your mom was close to my mom too, but we can't ask her." He slid his hand into his pocket and pulled out his cell phone. "I'll call her and see what she remembers. If she can be of help, we can stop and see her before we leave town."

"Leave town? She lives here?"

"I convinced her to come to Minnesota a few months after we settled here. Maverick was picking up work from us when he was on leave from the military and it seemed logical for her to be here, too. She's the last family we have and I wanted her close." He unlocked the phone screen and scrolled down to her number. "It's been over a year now that she's been dating again. He's an electrician and things are starting to get serious. Now that Maverick is out of the service, he's settled down here as well. Family is important and having them close by means more now than it did when I was younger because I know what the loss is like."

"Losing someone close to you makes you cling to those who are still there with you. For months after Mom died, I was terrified anytime Jay left the house. I thought he'd end up dead just like Mom. Fear controlled me so much that I followed him once."

"I bet Jay was pissed if he found out."

"Pissed doesn't begin to cover it. I'd never seen him so mad at me." She let out a deep sigh. "That's when I realized he was running drugs. He wasn't the dealer on the corner as he had done while he was in school. He was bigger than that. He had others working for him, doing the actual dealings."

"It wasn't just drugs." He held her tighter to him, as if he was worried she'd pull away. "Guns were another big money maker for him. Anything illegal he could get his hands in, he'd do it. That's when I realized I had to sever my connection to him. Callaway, Cain, and Cyrus were underage; they needed me. As their legal guardian, I couldn't risk involvement with him."

"But you were still there for him. You bailed him out of jail; you hired lawyers for him."

"No, Syd, not for him." His gaze locked on hers for a moment as she realized what he was saying. "It was always for you. You couldn't stay there alone with your father and once he was in prison, Jay was all you had. I considered letting him rot in jail but that meant you'd be put in the foster care system and I didn't want that for you."

"Thank you." She cupped the side of his face, dragging her fingers along the light stubble of his five-o'clock shadow. "Even though you weren't there, you were still thinking of me. Your actions prove it."

"I thought of you every day. Each morning I'd wake up, shut off the alarm, and see the picture of us together, and that picture was the last thing

I saw before I went to sleep. You were a part of my thoughts every day." He tipped his head and kissed the palm of her hand. "You've always held my heart; it just wasn't until recently that I discovered you're the woman I want to share the rest of my life with."

"I've known you were the man I wanted to spend my life with since I was six years old." She slipped her leg over his waist and climbed on top of him so her body was straddling his. "Mom told me to be patient and one day I'd have all my heart's desires. Patience was never my strong suit but she was right: it paid off. I got you."

"I'm glad you see it that way." He looped his arm around her back and brought her closer, chest to chest.

"Patience is about to pay off in another way." Reaching down between them, she grabbed the hem of her shirt before quickly pulling it over her head. "While we didn't get to have sex on your old desk before it was hauled away, there's new office furniture that needs to be broken in. I think we've waited long enough."

"I guess it's a good thing Cay is taking the business call at the house instead of in my office." He glanced at the phone he was still holding with his aunt's phone number on the display, waiting for him to press the call button. "Shouldn't we force our patience to last just a little bit longer and let me make this call first?"

"No. Whatever we learn won't change anything. If Anthony is my father, then he's dead so it's a closed door; and if he's not, then it still leads me to wondering who. I'm not sure I really care anymore. The man I've always thought was my father and both my brothers are criminals, each of them with blood on their hands…I guess the idea there may be another man who could be my biological father is a weight lifted off my shoulders. Perhaps I'm better than them because I'm not them. I guess I'd like to live with the hope they're no relation to me for a little bit longer."

"Then let's not waste any more time." He dropped the phone onto the sofa cushion and tipped his head, motioning for her to get up.

She hopped off him and headed toward the stairs, slipping out of the rest of her clothes as she did, and leaving a trail for him to follow. "Come on, handsome."

"You better hope no one's in my office," he teased as he followed her, his own tie and shirt already discarded.

"What?" She paused on the steps, just before she would have disappeared out of sight, and glanced back at him.

"I'm teasing." Catching up to her, he lifted her into his arms, pressing her naked body against his chiseled chest. "Everyone is over at the house. Cay was the last one hanging around, but he left before I came up here. We're alone."

"Jerk." She smacked her hand off his chest. "You had me terrified I'd walk naked into your office and find one of your brothers there. I could have never looked at them again."

"Don't worry, baby. I'd have killed them for catching a glimpse of my girl naked."

He carried her down the rest of the steps as her thoughts continued to circle around the way he'd said *my girl*. She still couldn't believe she was finally with him. An official couple. For years, she'd dreamed of him, but to actually have him in her life like he was still shocked her.

"Don't get lost in your thoughts."

"I wouldn't be taken out of this moment kicking and screaming. I've been looking forward to it since we ordered the furniture." As they stepped into the office, she looked at the matching dark maple executive desks with the black drawer handles and black leather office chairs to match. The only item on top of the desk was the office phone. Everything was still stacked on the filing cabinet that ran along the back wall, waiting for them to put things where they belonged. "I'm sorry."

"What baby?"

"If it wasn't for me, we'd have the office back in working order and Cay wouldn't be covering for you."

He lowered her down onto the top of the desk. "Don't, Syd. None of this is your fault. You're more important to me and Cay's capable of handling things. As for the office not being set up yet, it's all for the better; this way we don't have to move anything. I can have you spread out over the desks...or fuck, I think we need to do it on both desks. I'll have you screaming my name every which way and there won't be a single inch of this office that won't remind you of tonight."

"Promises." She shot him a cocky grin. Maybe it was because she was willing to forget about everything but them for a few hours, or maybe part of her believed him—either way it didn't matter.

"Let me show you." Without giving her a chance to respond, he pressed his lips to hers. Slipping his tongue between her lips, he devoured her, forcing her to arch into him.

"You're overdressed." She hooked her fingers in the waistband of his dress slacks.

"Don't worry, baby. I'm planning on losing them soon. Don't think, just feel." He kissed along her jawline until he reached the sweet spot just below her ear.

"I feel..." She let out a soft moan as his cool breath brushed along her flushed skin moments before his teeth grazed along her neck. "Your pants...material. I want you naked."

The feeling of being overwhelmed and lost in a sea of emotions were gone now that she was in his arms. She needed him like her next breath of air. He was her knight in shining armor and brought her back from the edge. He was her everything.

Claiming her nipple with his teeth, he scattered her thoughts. He teased the bud of her nipple between his teeth, gently tugging it until it hardened, and then moved over to the next one.

"Before you came into my life I never thought about making love on the desk but if you keep doing that, I'm going to take charge and you'll be on that chair with me riding you." She raked her nails lightly down the front of his chest and let her gaze linger on his. "Coal, I need you."

"You're so fucking sexy." He stripped out of his dress slacks and boxers in one quick move, letting them pool around his ankles before kicking them away. "My girl, you're awful cocky, thinking you can take over. This is my fantasy and I want you stretched out on this desk as I slide my cock deep in your pussy. Now lie back or I'm going to drag this out until you're fucking begging."

She leaned back on her elbows—wanting him right then. "Now you're too far away."

"Not for long." He grabbed her hips and slid her down the desk so she was barely on the edge. Only the fact that he was pressed up against the front of her kept her from sliding down onto the floor. "How's that?"

She reached out and touched his chest, slowly working her way down to his hardness—but the moment she teased along the edge of it, he grabbed a hold of her wrist.

"Not yet, baby."

Her gaze locked on to his. "Let me feel it. I want to wrap my hand around your dick and know that you're hard because of me." He let go of her wrist, arching his hips forward so his cock was easier for her to reach. Wrapping her fingers around it, she rubbed down the length, painstakingly slow, teasing just enough that he could feel her caresses without pain. "I

165

love that look in your eyes, the fire that burns within them, as if I'm the one that started it."

"You have, Syd. You most fucking certainly have."

She squeezed tighter around him as she worked down his length, causing him to let out a deep groan. "As good as this feels, and fuck it does, I want to be inside of you. I want to hear you scream my name as ecstasy engulfs you."

"Take me." Wanting that too, she let her hand fall away from him and leaned back so she was resting on both her elbows, her chest pushed out toward him. "I want you inside me now."

He slipped a finger between her folds and she arched up into his touch. "So wet for me."

"For you, only you, Coal." His name came out on a moan as his thumb brushed along her clit. "Please..."

Without waiting, he adjusted his angle, gliding his cock over her opening, and pulling a moan from her. Slowly, he glided the length of him inside, just a little at first, pulling a moan from deep within her as he worked his way inside her tight passage. Halfway in, he stopped and slid out, even as she leaned up and grabbed a hold of his hip, trying to force him to stay. Once he was out, he gripped her hips and slammed his length into her, filling her completely, rocking their bodies back and forth, each thrust gaining momentum.

She leaned back, hoping to grab the edge of the desk, but with them pressed together, there was nothing but smooth wood to grab. "Coal..." She moaned his name as he grabbed hold of her hips, pulling her down onto his cock and slamming into her. She arched toward him, thrusting her breasts toward him until he bent down and caught her nipple between his teeth. "Coal!" She screamed his name, not yet in orgasm but close to it when his teeth grazed along the sensitive bud.

With his tongue he drew small circles around the bud, blowing gently on it as he let it slip from between his lips. Without losing his rhythm, he dipped his head to catch the other one between his lips and do the same thing.

"So fucking beautiful." His voice sounded strained as if he was close to his own orgasm but was waiting for her to have her release first.

"Coal," she whispered, her climax within reach. "Faster, please…"

He did as she asked, his fingers digging into her hips and causing just enough pressure to be erotic, and sped up his pace. She wrapped her legs around him, locking her ankles together at the small of his back, keeping him from pulling back too far. Tension had her muscles constricting around him as her orgasm neared, urging him to engage an even faster rhythm, and his eyes glazed over with his own ecstasy creeping up on him.

Arching up toward him, she tangled her fingers in his longer strands, bringing his head down so she could claim his lips. Slipping her tongue in between his lips, she moaned his name as her release found her. With her free hand she raked the skin along the arch of his shoulders, digging her nails into his flesh.

Then he broke the kiss and slammed into her one final time before leaning forward against her and letting go, filling her. "Fuck, baby."

Chapter Sixteen

Days turned into weeks and weeks into months. Somehow, through it all, Sydney began to accept her past to build the future she wanted. Everything that had happened had brought her to this place in her life and this thought was enough to keep her pushing forward. She was happy where she was and with Coal being a part of her life. She'd never expected to end up here but now that she had him, she wasn't about to let anything divide her from her happiness, especially not her own hang ups or her family.

After speaking with Betsy, Coal's aunt, she'd learned that the man she had called Dad all her life wasn't her biological father. Anthony was the one. Betsy and her mother had been good friends and her mother had confided in her about Anthony and her thoughts about filing for divorce. Thanks to this friendship, Sydney had been able to learn more than she had expected and this gave her some peace. She was more thankful for the past friendship between the women when Coal's search into Anthony's past had revealed a bunch of dead ends. He had been left on the church steps as an infant, so there was no family for her to find to prove this latest revelation.

Even knowing that her father was dead and there was no family to locate, this was enough for her. She embraced Betsy's news and allowed it to give her a whole new lease on life. Maybe she was willing to believe this fantasy blindly because it was a way to disconnect with her father, Tim, and their crimes. There had been a moment of pain when she realized disconnecting from them would disconnect her from Jay, as well. That was until she remembered everything he had done to get her into this mess. She'd loved Jay but it was just too much and he was gone.

"I heard you were a hit with Hawk." Cay strolled toward her, a stack of papers in hand. "From what I hear, he wants to only deal with you in the future and that's high praise coming from him. Before you, he wouldn't work with anyone but Coal. Heck, he barely tolerates me."

"Talking on the phone to Hawk, I'd have never guessed he had such a sweetheart side to him. He's an old charmer."

"I'd laugh at that comment but Coal told me about it. I'd have said that man didn't have a sweet ounce in him. I guess it was in hiding until you came along to bring it out." Cay tossed the papers onto the corner of her desk. "Orders for some of the new projects Cal and I are working on."

"I'll get them done today." She reached over and slid the papers toward her as he lingered near the desk. "What's on your mind?"

"Cain." The name of the second youngest Tanner brother came out softly as if he was expecting her to shut him down before giving him a chance to voice his concerns. "He's been closed off from all of us for too long. I'm just…"

"Worried about him?" she finished when his words died off.

"Yeah." He leaned on the corner of her desk. "He doesn't talk to any of us. Not really."

"And you want me to tell you if you should be concerned about him." She paused for a moment, hoping he'd deny it but he didn't. "I can tell you he's not a danger to himself or others. He's been alone for so long, locked in his own self-imposed prison that part of him seems to have forgotten what it's like to be around people. He blames himself for what happened and part of the way he's dealt with it was by withdrawing. He feels he

170

robbed you and Coal of your chance at a carefree young adult lifestyle. Coal was twenty-three and you had just turned twenty-one. The two of you should have been out partying, having a good time. Especially you. Instead, Coal stepped up to take responsibility for his three minor brothers: Cal, Cain, and Cyrus. You were right there with him. The two of you not only raised those boys, but you made this shop a success as well."

"It's what family does. We band together." Cay made it sound so simple when she knew first hand that wasn't always the case. Some families didn't give a shit about the other members of the family. "What can we do for him?"

"Give him time." She placed her hand on Cay's. "From what I've gathered, this is the first time Cain has reached out to anyone since the accident. Don't force yourself on him. Continue doing what you were doing, visiting him occasionally, but don't overwhelm him or he's likely to retreat into himself again. Even when you feel like we're making no progress, we must continue to move at his pace."

"What is it about you that will make him come out of his cabin? He's willing to confide in you when he shuts the rest of us out." Cay's voice sounded almost pained.

"I'm an outsider."

"Bullshit." Cay pulled his hand out from under hers and rose from where he was perched on the corner of her desk. "You've always been part of this family. You and Jay were over for dinner at least twice a week while we were growing up. You were always hanging around. Now…well, let's just say you're even more a part of this family. I haven't seen Coal this happy in years and that's your doing."

"Then maybe Cain is able to speak with me about things he hasn't been able to with you because…" She paused because suddenly the words that were coming out of her mouth sounded rude and too harsh.

"Because it wasn't your father's head he had on his lap." Cay stalked toward the window. "After he pulled Mom from the wreckage, he went after your mother. He was just pulling her out of the flames when the fire department showed up. He tried with them but with Dad…"

"There was nothing he could have done." Her voice was too soft as she fought the memories that wanted to descend on her. Even as she fought the emotions, she could see the crime scene photos flashing in her mind. Mr. Tanner had been decapitated; she didn't know what had caused it, but his head had landed in Cain's lap. She couldn't picture anything more horrible than to have that happen and her heart went out to Cain. "He did everything he could for both your mom and mine."

"But it wasn't enough. Both ended up dead."

"The blame for that falls on Tim, not Cain. My brother is the one who tore apart both our families." She pushed her chair back from the desk. "Cain could have died that night too but he survived, and for that, we should all be grateful."

"I'm grateful." Coal strolled into the room, his gaze falling on his brother. "Scared but alive."

"He retreated from the family because he blames himself for what happened. If he hadn't knocked the shit out of Nelson after he forced himself on Ginny, your parents wouldn't have been out that night. Nelson was supposed to give him a ride home after the game and pizza."

"Nelson deserved to get his ass kicked." Cay shook his head. "Besides that Cain isn't to blame for what happened. Fuck, he could have been killed that night, too. Risking himself, he tried to save the others."

"Give him a little time," Sydney encouraged. "There's no magic cure for everything he has been through but he's working through it. I think he wants to make changes, but again I say if you all rush him, then he's going to get overwhelmed quickly and go back in his shell."

"Will you alert us if you think he's dangerous?" Cay watched her closely.

"Cay." Coal's voice held a touch of warning.

"What aren't you telling me?" She pushed, knowing there was something Cay was concerned with but Coal was trying to keep quiet. "Don't shut me out. If you want my help with this, I need to know. I've spent some time with him lately, maybe more time than any of you have recently, so if there's something I need to be concerned about you need to tell me."

"She's right, Coal. She needs to know."

"Damn you, Cay. Why can't you let this shit go?" Anger filled Coal's voice as he glared at his brother.

"Because if there's a chance she's right then we have to keep him from acting on his impulses."

"Coal?" She rose from the desk and went to stand next to him. "You know me. I'm not going to judge. Hell, I have no right to judge even if I would—look at the shit I've come from. We've been through a lot together and I care about Cain as much as you do. Let me help."

"Get back to work," he snapped at Cay but his gaze found hers and softened slightly.

"You need to—"

"Don't tell me what I need to do." He tore his gaze from her to look over at Cay. "You should have spoken with me before coming to Syd."

"It wasn't planned; it just happened." Cay gave one last look at her as if silently telling her to press the subject until his brother told her the truth, before he strolled out of the office leaving them alone.

"Coal." She reached out and placed her hand on his chest. "Whatever it is, you can tell me."

"Do you know what Hawk said about you? He said you were a smooth talker. During that business meeting, you had him like putty in your hands."

"I don't understand what that has to do with Cain."

"Not Cain, baby." He took hold of her hand and brought it to his lips, placing a soft kiss on her knuckles. "Me, baby, I'm putty in your hands and when you look at me like that, how can I hide anything from you?"

"Then don't hide anything from me. Nothing you tell me is going to scare me away. I love you, Coal, and I care about Cain. Honestly, I never expected to develop such a friendship with him, but something about it seems too easy. If I had developed that with any of your brothers, I would have thought it would have been Cyrus since we were already friendly when we were kids."

"But there's tension between you and Cyrus because he had hoped your arrival here might open a romantic relationship door for the two of you."

"I know he thought that but there could have never been anything between us. He's attractive but my heart has always belonged to another. Now stop trying to change the subject." She didn't pull her hand out of his as much as changed the way he was holding it so their fingers interlaced. "Why is Cay so concerned about Cain?"

"After the accident, Cain was different. There was something dark to him. Anger fueled him until there was nothing else left within him. It got so bad, he couldn't attend school. We had him on homebound where a teacher would come here and work with him so he would graduate. His anger would send him off like a rocket for no reason and no warning. It was too dangerous to allow him to be around other children. I was concerned about him being around the rest of my brothers, but what could I do? I couldn't send him away. Instead, I sent him to therapy."

"When I speak with him now, I don't see anger fueling him. He's lost and there's a darkness to him but I wouldn't say there's rage controlling him."

"About a year ago, things started to change and we've been trying harder to get him involved in family activities. He's reserved still but he at least allows us inside the cabin now. Before this, no one besides me could make it past the threshold. He'll let you know when he's had enough and then it's time to go. He's witnessed too much…" As he stared down at her, his eyes held unspoken sadness and she wrapped her arms around him, offering him what little comfort she could. No words could take away the past or erase the memories that plagued Cain. "The therapist believed his rage would lead him to become dangerous. She was concerned he'd act on the memories and seek revenge, except the person who was responsible was out of reach. Because of that, she believed his rage might strike out at anyone close to him. That it would control him, instead of him controlling it. She recommended we commit him for inpatient therapy, but we'd already lost so much. Before we did something so drastic, we wanted to get a second opinion."

"And did you?" she pressed.

"Yes. Doctor Webster—he'd worked with Cain until he was eighteen, at which time I could no longer force him to continue his therapy. Doctor Webster didn't agree with the first doctor about Cain being a threat to anyone or the inpatient therapy route. If Cain is a threat to anyone, it's to himself. His withdrawal is depriving him of so much but you can't force someone to participate in life." He rubbed his hand along the curve of her back. "Cain isn't a threat to you or I would have never allowed him near you."

"You did tell me to stay away from him when we first arrived."

"I wasn't sure how he'd react. I didn't think he'd attack you, but I was concerned he'd retreat further into himself. Your presence could have served as a trigger to remind him of past trauma." He tightened his grip around her waist, drawing her closer. "I never dreamed his reaction would have been as it has. You can't blame me for wanting to protect both of you."

"I can't but I still wish you would have told me how bad things had been with Cain. I don't know if I'm helping or hurting him by spending time with him."

"Helping," he reassured her. "I've seen the two of you together. There's an ease I wish I had with him. In the last five years, he hasn't interacted with the rest of us as much he has in the last couple of weeks. Whatever you're doing is working. Every once in a while, I see a glimpse of the old Cain coming out. Do you have any idea how happy that makes me?"

"I think so because it makes me happy too. The friendship developing between Cain and me is something that for most people takes years to build but for us it's happened in a matter of weeks. I never would have suspected something like this could happen. He's a good man and with all of us by his side I think he can make progress."

He took her hand in his and stepped back toward the sofa before taking a seat and quickly pulling her down onto his lap. "It seems like so long ago since I found you in your childhood bedroom, ready to shoot me."

"It was only a few months ago." She settled back against the arm of the sofa so she could look at him and he kept his arm still loose around her waist, his fingers brushing along the curve of her hip.

"I know but it seems like a lifetime ago. I had planned to keep you at arm's length, never allowing myself to get too close to you because I was worried I wouldn't be able to let you go if I did. Now I know I was right."

"I'm not going anywhere."

"I can't imagine not holding you in my arms at night as we both drift off to sleep, or not waking next to you each morning. Sharing an office with anyone was not something I'd ever expected to do, but looking up to see you sitting across from me and knowing you care about this company as much as I do is truly special. I love you, Sydney Manor, and I never want to spend a moment without you in it. Will you marry me?"

"Aren't you supposed to be down on one knee?" She raised an eyebrow at him.

"I wanted to do it right here in the place where I knew I was a goner. Kneeling on the sofa proposing...well, let's just say that would have been classical but I highly doubt romantic. Though if you'd like I'd get down on one knee and do it the way you always dreamed up."

"You already have." She looped her arms around his neck. "All I've ever hoped for is that my childhood proposal would come true. Now I guess since we've each asked each other, we can finally live happily ever after."

"Is that a yes?" He slipped his hand into the pocket of his pants and pulled out a small box. Moments later, he had a beautiful rose gold engagement ring in his hand. The main diamond that had to be more than a carat was expertly carved into a beautiful princess cut, with two smaller diamonds on each side to match.

"Yes, Coal Tanner, I will marry you." She watched as he slid the ring on her finger. "I'm going to make you the happiest man alive."

"You already have." Sealing the proposal, he tangled his hand into her hair and drew her in for a kiss. "I love you, Syd." His breath brushed along her skin before he closed the small distance between them and claimed her lips.

Marissa Dobson

Born and raised in the Pittsburgh, Pennsylvania area, Marissa Dobson now resides about an hour from Washington, D.C. She's a lady who likes to keep busy, and is always busy doing something. With two different college degrees, she believes you are never done learning.

Being the first daughter to an avid reader, this gave her the advantage of learning to read at a young age. Since learning to read she has always had her nose in a book. It wasn't until she was a teenager that she started writing down the stories she came up with.

Marissa is blessed with a wonderful supportive husband, Thomas. He's her other half and allows her to stay home and pursue her writing. He puts up with all her quirks and listens to her brainstorm in the middle of the night.

Her writing buddy Pup Cameron, a cocker spaniel, is always around to listen to her bounce ideas off him. He might not be able to answer, but they're helpful in their own ways.

She loves to hear from readers so send her an email at marissa@marissadobson.com or visit her online at http://www.marissadobson.com.

Other Books by Marissa Dobson

Alaskan Tigers:

Tiger Time

The Tiger's Heart

Tigress for Two

Night with a Tiger

Trusting a Tiger

Alaskan Tigers Box Set Volume One

Jinx's Mate

Two for Protection

Bearing Secrets

Tiger Tracks

Healing the Clan

Alaskan Tigers Box Set Volume Two

Her Black Tiger

Forever Creek Shifters:

Forever Fight

Crimson Hollow:

Romancing the Fox

Loving the Bears

A Lion's Chance

Swift Move

Purrable Lion

Bearly Alive

Saved by a Lion

Stormkin:

Storm Queen

Reaper:

A Touch of Death

SEALed for You:

Ace in the Hole

Explosive Passion

Operation Family

Marine for You:

Lucky Chance

Back from Hell

A Marines Second Chance *Crossover to the SEALed for You series

Tanner Cycles:

Until Sydney

Beyond Monogamy:

Theirs to Treasure

Cedar Grove Medical:

Hope's Toy Chest

Destiny's Wish

Leena's Dream

Fate:

Snowy Fate

Sarah's Fate

Mason's Fate

As Fate Would Have It

Half Moon Harbor Resort:

Learning to Live

Learning What Love Is

Her Cowboy's Heart

Half Moon Harbor Resort Volume One

Clearwater:

Winterbloom

Unexpected Forever

Losing to Win

Christmas Countdown

The Surrogate

Clearwater Romance Volume One

Small Town Doctor

Stand Alone:

SEALed Rescue

SEALed in Texas

Through Smoke

Through Fire

Starting Over

Secret Valentine

Restoring Love

www.ingramcontent.com/pod-product-compliance
Lightning Source LLC
Chambersburg PA
CBHW022111170626
46808CB00002B/691